CW00958353

THE DREAMLESS

Rosete Rodrigues

authorHOUSE®

AuthorHouse™ UK
1663 Liberty Drive
Bloomington, IN 47403 USA
www.authorhouse.co.uk
Phone: UK TFN: 0800 0148641 (Toll Free inside the UK)
UK Local: (02) 0369 56322 (+44 20 3695 6322 from outside the UK)

Published by AuthorHouse 02/28/2024

ISBN: 979-8-8230-8338-6 (sc)
ISBN: 979-8-8230-8339-3 (hc)
ISBN: 979-8-8230-8340-9 (e)

Library of Congress Control Number: 2023911534

Print information available on the last page.

This book is printed on acid-free paper.

(Army had reached the last of us already destroyed inside.
She had screamed and run and tried to hide, but what Army
didn't know was that no matter how hard she tried to
keep the distance, He would always be one step
ahead of her. It would be her shadow...
Then Army dropped a last tear with the fragment of her soul,
looked at the sky and closed her eyes. With the strength she had
left, Army screamed, and the Gates of Wisdom opened.
That's when we saw our way back to Timeless.)

#Wrath

GREEDINESS

(I was the one who saw tomorrow rush towards us, but it came and came stronger and more enthralling than ever.)

Right after that, everything had taken a different turn. Each one had plunged into their own regrets...
...Apart from me all others have succumbed to the depths of their sins.
He let us go to the other side, but I was the only one left behind.
I had anticipated something like this would happen and I wasn't able to stop it.

Everything collapsed like a house of cards. Everything collapsed with a simple breath, in a turbulent night, where all our inner and outer selves were in war. I wish I could say something, scream at least, but... I couldn't do anything to get us out of this disgrace.
The hot summer days, where the sun reflected our darker side, were remembered in the photographic memories I had recorded, but now all that was gone.

These days? Now they were rainy, where even the rain that cleansed our souls and filled us with nostalgia, became the source of my deepest regret. I was fighting this alone. They left and on the one hand I also wanted to go, I wanted to be with them, but... If I had gone, I don't know if I would have survived this, but... even if I stayed I would have lost them forever....

What was the point of me regretting? I was already one of them. I was like them now. Just me and my biggest regret now transformed me, in my greatest sin... into what I am today... A mortal sin...

Today was one of those days. Rainy, where not even the gray sky conveyed peace, only nostalgia, rancor, sorrow...
Sitting on one of the benches in one of the parks not too far or too close to where I now live, in the rain, watching people walk past me as if they had never seen me. They ignored me or looked at me as if I were a being from another world.
- People are more afraid of what they see than what they can't see. Difference is humanity's greatest enemy. -who was?

I looked to the side and saw her. She didn't look at me, she looked at people, she was wet, completely wet, like me.
I've sat on this stool forever, since everything had ended with us completely... It was hard to count time when you didn't notice it, and in all that time, no one had ever stopped for more than two seconds to look at me, to reject me, let alone sit beside me.

- Who are you? -I asked her.
- I'm just someone sitting in the rain while trying to understand the human mind.
- I've never seen you around here.
- But I've seen you around here, always in the same place, on the same bench...
- Yeah. - I looked at the floor.
- Where do you live?
- I had no place in this world for a long time.
- You speak as if you've lived all this time.
- And I lived. But for me life stopped passing by.
- It passes, you're the one who stopped living it.
- How can I live knowing that others stopped living because of me?
- Who?
- All of them are gone and if I had followed in their footsteps, I might have been with them right now.

- Died? -looked at me.
- They're lost somewhere. Maybe I'm dead to them.
- You're alive, right here... You're real, I can see you. – could she?
- Because?
- Because you're different. Unique and I know you see the world the same way I do.
- How do you know that?
- I don't know, but I feel, and I trust my heart.
- You're a strange person. What name do you carry?
- What's my name is that? Army and you?
- Me?
-Yes. -She smiled. A genuine, angelic smile, perfect for her.
- I didn't have a name for some time.
- So, what do you want me to call you.
- They named me Gluttony.
- Who?
- The one who once gave me a second chance.
- I did not understand. Strange speech.
- The regret. I tried to fight him, but I always lost, even before it started.
- Coming? - She stood up and held out her hand.

I looked at both, at her hand and then at her.
- Don't bother with me, you can go on with your life.
- That's what I'm doing.
- Maybe it would be easier to forget that you saw me, as others do. They just walk by and leave me alone, it's like I don't exist for them.
- I tried, but these eyes, this outfit... I don't know... it's as if all this attracted me. Like a magnet.
- I am sorry.
- Because?
- For not being perfect.
- Gluttony?
- I said...-maybe if I hadn't answered I would still be in the same place as before. Sitting on my bench in the rain while confirming that I'm unwanted by the people.

We were already out of the park, and she was holding my hand and walking me along the sidewalk.
Strangely her hand was warm, even though it was wet, maybe for less time than me, but her hand was still warm.

I almost couldn't think, and barely processing what was happening. People continued to look at us strangely.
- Why did you stop? -I asked. I asked? My question was puzzled, and she looked at me with bulging eyes, perhaps also surprised by my question.
- It stopped raining. -she looked up at the sky as a beautiful, radiant smile drew on her lips.

It might have been a gray day, but it was like a star had fallen right in front of me.
- Truth. -I also looked up.
- Let's go?
- Where? I want to know where you're taking me. Only that. -I tried to justify my question.
- Let's go to a beautiful place.
- Nothing looks pretty in this weather. It was once beautiful, but it was no longer so long ago. Where days like this made people happy.
- I like to hear you talk. You experienced something wonderful, I'm sure of it.
- I lost all certainty. The days were wonderful, but... -the bells began to ring. – I need to go.
- Where?
- Somewhere. I must go. Forget you ever saw me; forget you ever spoke to me. Forget everything that happened. Forget this day.

Army#

He was gone. As fast as the blink of an eye... Gluttony. What name.
I didn't know what had happened in his past to be like this, but he regretted it every day.

Those sunset-colored eyes, so peculiar and mesmerizing and at the same time, it made me lose reality. His white shirt, black dress pants and some sandals. Chocolate brown hair and eyeglasses. Too much perfection for one person.

I walked back to the park hoping to find him again, but no one was there. He was really gone.
I eagerly awaited his coming.

I decided to go home, but all the way I did it was with that being inside my thoughts. He was like the Full Moon. Full of regrets and sorrow. Maybe if I looked for the people he had lost in the past, some joy would settle inside him and make him a New Moon.

Maybe I understood what Gluttony was going through. Fears, pain, regrets... all this kills the human being from the inside.
It would be hard to find his home or him, but someone as peculiar as he doesn't go unnoticed.

It was decided, tomorrow I would look for the person who invaded my thoughts to the point of giving me something to accomplish. A goal, a dream, a wish. A desire... the desire to want to make a difference, to be different at all costs. I wanted to give you back the life you lost.

I showered, ate dinner, and made my list of possible possibilities of going right or wrong.
More decided it was impossible to be and no one was going to change my mind.

Greediness#

How this life weighs. How heavy it is on my back.
I was at home... better… in the place I came to call "home."
- At home? How was your day? - he asked.

He's been with me from the beginning. I don't know his name. I never saw his face, but it was him who one day found me lost and welcomed me. It was him who had led me to repentance, and he had baptized me with that name.
I fell into the temptation of the delights he cooked, nothing better than drowning my sorrows in food.

I had once cooked for those who were lost by my indecision.
- Yes. The day is still rainy.
- It doesn't rain anymore.
- No, but the pain continues, it doesn't stop. I just stopped feeling something when...
- When?
- Nothing. I'm going to shower and then I'm going to dinner. Prepare my meal.
- It's already prepared. I will serve you. Don't be long before it cools down.
- I'll do it. Place all the seats at the table. -I passed him and walked towards my room.

Storyteller#

Gluttony entered his room and stopped at the first frame. Only he appeared in it, in the center and the rest was just the shadow. If anyone else was in that photograph, it was gone. Maybe it was the people he had lost in the past. Maybe it was who he most wants to meet again.
Various frames in the same way, where only he appeared smiling, distorted his reality and increased his hurts and regrets.

After he had bathed, he wore a silk shirt in sunset orange and pants of the same fabric in black. A pair of leather shoes and a feathered cloak, not forgetting his glasses.

His "servant" or "steward" was waiting for him at the table where six more seats were set.

Gluttony had sat in the main chair and waited to be served.
Even wanting to go back, dying inside because of his choices in the past, Gluttony succumbed to his own sin.
He had long ago allowed to discern which was his reality or the reality that surrounded him.

He had subjected himself to a life of punishment for himself and had already lost any hope of ever getting well.
- Bring me more... No, bring me my dessert.
- But sir...
- Bring it! I know what I do. Don't question what I say. Just do what I tell you and bring it... - he shouted.

The servant said nothing more, just followed his instructions and went to prepare more food for Gluttony but stopped halfway and looked at his master before smiling.
On the other hand, Gluttony was in a trance. He had placed everything that was seconds away on the table, on the floor. He had pulled out the towel, dragging her with him to the door, not even looking back for a second. And there he left it, along with the tableware.

Greediness#

I walked to the door and headed towards my room.
This wasn't me. It wasn't the same as before. He had ceased to be such a long time ago. In a past where the present of now an uncertain future was before.
It had ceased to be after he had freed him from that torture.
Inside my room I walked to my bed and in it I released the weight of my exhaustion, sank into it, and closed my eyes.

Storyteller#

It was already morning; Army had been up for a long time and was ready to begin her mission.
To be different it didn't rain, the sky was almost blue, but you could still see some gray clouds, lining up.
Back at the park where she always watched Gluttony, Army sat on the bench where he used to sit.

After some time of waiting he appears, but soon changed course after seeing her.
- Wait. I need to talk to you. -she got up and followed him.
- I don't know who you are or what you want from me.
- Gluttony?
- I asked you to forget about me. I asked you to forget that you ever spoke to me. I asked you all that and you ignored it. -he spoke loudly.
- Yes, but you also said to live my life and that's what...
- Don't disturb me. - he turned suddenly, and Army was scared by him.
- I need to talk to you.
- There's nothing you have to say that interests me.
- How do you know that?
- Because... I just want you to ignore me like everyone else. Pretend you don't know me.
- Because? I can help you find them again... I know someone who can help us. I want to help...
- Stop ... - he shouted, and she was frightened once more.

Everyone was stopped to watch, but soon dispersed. Granted, it didn't interest them.
- Comes. - she held out her hand once more.
- I'm just asking you to leave me. Forget me. -she turned her back on him and just walked aimlessly.
- I am unable. I tried to forget that I ever saw you, but you invaded my thoughts from the moment I looked you in the eye. From the moment I saw it for a second, even though it was small, however small it was, I saw it in your eyes. -she walked behind him while holding her nightgown.

- What did you see? Sadness? Hurt? Repentance? - he stopped walking and she did the same.
- No... I saw hope. I saw relief... -Gula was face to face with her.
- What relief? What hope?
- Why not?
- What do you really want?
- Like this? I don't understand. -she replied.

Gluttony had approached her, and Army had retreated until there was no more room to retreat.
- I'm asking what you really want in relation to me?
- I don't know what you want to know, but I need you to be more specific.
- I do not trust you. I've never seen you and suddenly you enter mine... and decide to change everything according to your preferences? Who are you really? Who sent you?
- You can think what you want...
- I think. Believes so. - he asked leaning against the wall preventing her from running away, as she planned to do.
- I thought you were different from this...
- Do you think? -he smiled. - I just like to make sure no one hides ulterior motives. - he tilted his head to the side and looked deep into her peculiar, intriguing eyes. It wasn't the color itself; it was the way she looked that made him feel something different.

- Everything is fine. I understand that you think everything of me, but can you at least give me a chance to explain myself? I can show you who I really am and show...
- Don't go there. - interrupted her. - Let's start with you. Prove to me that I must not harm you. I've never tasted human flesh, but who knows? - He approached her closer and smiled in an evil way.
- It's a lie, right? - She was terrified.
- Of course, yes. Who do you think I am? I may have been abducted for evil, but I still think for myself. - he had said and then walked away. She sighed deeply and looked up at the sky.

- You know? I also felt something different when I spoke to you yesterday, but...
- Are you afraid?
- Don't go there.
- Sorry. -she smiled.
- Let's go?
- Where? -she was confused.
- I thought you wanted to show me who you really are, besides if I remember correctly yesterday you wanted me to see something. I am wrong?
- No. I thought you had forgotten about that...
- I can change my mind if you prefer...
- No! All right, let's go then. - She smiled and stepped forward in front of him.
- What's in that bag?
- This?
- That's what I asked.
- Sure, sorry. That's all we're going to need. I knew you would change your mind. – She was smiling again.
- Did you knew?
- No, but I wanted to prevent it. Let's go?

Army#

I was happy, so happy that the happiness almost overflowed.
We walked to a garden, where there were lots of flowers. It was gorgeous to die for, metaphorically, of course.

I had taken some photographs to remember. He was sitting in the shade while eating the fruit that was on the trees. It felt like paradise.
Without him noticing I took the opportunity to make a wreath of flowers to offer him later, but the bells were already ringing loudly and according to his name, Gluttony, even without saying it I would still be hungry.
- I'm leaving.
- Where?
- Feed myself. The rest of a good day.

- You just ate.
- I'm not satisfied. I'm leaving.
- Come with me? -he stopped.
- Where?
- Surprise. Are you coming?
- I need to feed. When you're done, meet me at the park and I'll go with you.
- I already smell it. I can imagine the immense variety of food, from heaven and earth to the ocean. -I smiled imagining the face he was making. - Can you feel it?
- Maybe I can go see what it is. If it doesn't take long. - he said seriously looking to the side.
- All right. Deal. -laughs.
- I can always change...
- You will not. I already stopped.

It was still difficult to understand what was going on inside Gluttony's head, but it was fun.

As soon as we arrived at the place, he almost fainted from so much emotion, but he wasn't expressing it by acts, you could see it in his eyes. It was a wooden cabin, very spacious. An open-air restaurant. There were a few people, but not many. In the center a table full of food from the most varied dishes, as I said before, from heaven and earth to the sea.

- Army my dear, you're here. I knew you would come... Who is this charming boy? Boyfriend? - Lux asked as soon as he saw him.
- No. Just a friend.
- Know. -he smiled and winked at me. - Come on, you can eat whatever you want. -He directed us to a table, and we sat down.
- What are you going to eat...? -I asked, but he was already up. - All right.
- Army?
- Yea?
- Can you come here for a moment?
- Of course. -I got up and went to Lux.

Lux was like a father to me. He has been with me since I know myself. He had already lived a long time and had seen unimaginable things, better than anyone he knew how to help Gluttony.
- Yea?
- What's he doing here?
- Gluttony?
- Since when do you know him?
- For some time, I have seen him lost in his own thoughts. I decided to help him. So, I thought... There is no one better than you to do it. But why do you ask? Do you know him?
- Yes. He is one of Pandora's sons and the sixth prince of the Universe.
- Do you think you can help him?
- Of course, I can, but it's not me he needs...
- Me?
- Who else would it be? He's here for you.
- But what if he doesn't want my help...?
- You can't eat more; you've already eaten enough.
- Who decides that? As far as I know, hunger belongs to me, I decide whether I am satisfied or not. Understood? -Gluttony was arguing with a man.
- There are more people who also came to eat, you're not the only one who came for lunch...
- As I already said, I'm the one who decides whether or not I should eat more, and I'm still not satisfied. Now if you don't mind, get out of my way. - It really wasn't happy at all.
- Gluttony? Let's go. -I approached him and gently touched his hand, but a kind of shock made me push it away.
- What do you think you're doing? I'm not leaving here until I finish my meal. -he replied decisively and seriously.
- You can eat elsewhere...
- You're the one who brought me... Rules?
- I know, but first you need to calm down.
- I'm calm.
- you don't seem calm.
- It's not my problem. -he replied and took a deep breath with his eyes closed.

- Where are you going?
- Away, before regret overtakes me again. Don't bother me anymore. Don't follow me and pretend not to know me the next time you meet me. I'll do the same... By the way, who are you? -he was angry.

Gluttony had just left without even looking back.
- What are you going to do now? -asked Lux.
- I don't know.
- Are you going to give him up?
- I did not say that.
- But?
- I never thought helping someone was so complicated.
- I know and no one said it was easy.
- So, I need to find him.
- Leave him alone for now. He will come to you.
- All right. If you say so. Until later. - I said goodbye to him and went back home.

I didn't stop thinking about him for a single second. I wanted to know how he was and where he was or what he was doing right now, but I trusted Lux's words and would expect him to come to me. I doubted it a little bit, but I had faith.

I let myself sleep and woke up to the sound of the tolling.
I looked at the clock and it was almost six in the afternoon.
I got up and left the house. I ran through the streets towards somewhere. I didn't really know why I ran, but I had to go somewhere, that was for sure. Something called to me with force.

It took me a while to get there, but I finally stopped. I was dead tired; I could barely breathe.

It might be a little far away, but I could already hear the strength of his bravery. It was like it was at war with itself. Like Gluttony.
The sun wasn't shining much anymore, but even so, it waved us goodbye, together with the wind, which involved me with affection, the sand stroked my feet and the sea invited me for a hug, next to the rocks, deep inside.

He was standing in front of the sea, so I decided to go to him and put me side by side with Gluttony.
It was he who called me without a shadow of a doubt.

I looked at him and he had closed his eyes, maybe this place had brought him memories, the ones he tried so hard to forget.
- This is one of my favorite places. What do you think? -I asked him but he kept his eyes closed. I posed in my purse and pulled out my camera. I focused on him and took several pictures.
- I thought I was very clear.
- And you were, but I didn't even know where it was coming from, until I got here.
- What are you doing with that thing?
- I'm creating memories. Here. I held out my hand with the camera and he finally decided to look at me.
- Go away.
- Didn't you want to know who I am? Go ahead. Anytime you want. -after a long time, he took it and took a picture of me.

Greediness#

Why? Who was she? And why did it make me feel so intrigued? It was like repentance in person. It was as if the urge to consume her was taking over me...

I wanted her to be closer to me and never to go away. Like before. All those feelings, this place… it was as if I could feel them, but I knew it was a mere illusion.
Whenever I was with her, they seemed to be together and that somehow lessened my hurt and regret.
I had positioned myself once more to photograph her, while running after some birds that stopped there to feed... how could something like this be real?

I dropped the camera and dropped to my knees myself. The pain of loss consumed my body and made it as heavy as the strength of this immense ocean in front of me.

All the memories I had tried to forget, the same ones that are no longer found on the walls of that "room", where only I remained, remembering that I was now alone, drove me crazy.
- Gluttony? -she screamed. - What is it?
- Nothing. Is nothing. - I said with some difficulty.
- What do you feel?
- I feel strange, it's not the first time and it won't be the last, I confess. In the beginning it was less painful, but I always got over it alone and everything will go back to normal, so this time it will be like the others.
- How can you bear something like that alone? -Her voice was shaky.
-.... -I tried to speak, but the pain only increased, and I ended up lying down on the sand.
- Tell me, what's going on? Say something! -even being in pain I could see her clearly. Even with my eyes closed, her face was etched in my thoughts.

I felt something fall on my face.
- What are you doing? -I asked her before the pain disappeared in the next second.
- Nothing. - her voice was trembling. It was remarkable that something was going on. Still panting, I opened my eyes and saw something I never thought I would see.
- Why are you crying? -why?
- I don't know. -she wiped her face and smiled still sniffling. - You are fine?
- Yes, as I said the pain is gone.
- Why? -I had asked the same question, you just didn't hear it.
- Why what?
- Why do you always do that?
- Could you be more specific?
- Why is it that whenever I try to help, you stay away? I thought you were going to die and maybe I would die with you, from fear, if you hadn't told me, it had already happened, but still, how can you go through something like this alone?

- Yeah, I'm not trustworthy. I took them to ruin and now I'm paying for it. The sin is mine, you don't have to try to bear it.
- How can you say such a thing? We're friends. You're the first friend I make. I feel I can trust you...- I got up.
- Army? - someone had called her.
- Lux? What are you doing here?
- Are you well?
- Yes, why?
- Comes here.
- Why?
- Just do what I tell you. -she helped me up.
- Your Highness. -Army and I look back.
- Why are you here?
- I ask the same. I was worried about you, so I decided to come find you.
- I'm fine.
- Who is he? -she asked.
- Dark. -Dark? I looked at him but said nothing.
- What do you mean Dark? Do you know him? -Army asked Lux.

Army#

I thought it was strange that his name was Dark, and he knew Gluttony, but there's also Lux, I can't complain.
- Your Highness, we must go. -suggested Dark.
- Wait! -I asked him, but Dark had placed himself in front of me as soon as I took two steps.
- Stay away from him, you insult human. -excuse me?
- Because?
- Someone like you can never give him what he needs. -I don't like him. At all.

I took another step, and he was still in place.
- You owned the poor boy. -Lux spoke and walked towards Dark. - You were the one who condemned him to this life.
- What do you know?

- More than I wanted. I know you as well as I know myself or even better than that and I know what you're capable of.
- The same can I say. I will make your words mine, my dear...
- Gluttony? -I yelled after I saw him fall. – Gluttony?

I ran towards him and as before, Dark tried to stop me, but Lux intervened in my favor. It was the same as before, even knowing it would pass I couldn't help but worry.
- Gluttony? -I called him.
- It has never happened before. All my memories are at war. I want them to stop.
- Tell me what you see!
- I had lived that moment. The moment when the seven of us were in a place identical to this one, where only we had fun like tomorrow was never going to come, but it had come and everything happened too fast.

There was again that feeling of wanting to die, not to feel that way. I don't understand why I can never keep my distance.

Whenever it's just me and him, whenever I touch him, there's always this closeness that leaves me almost without strength. His eye color was more intense. They glowed brighter than ever; it was like they were the sunset itself. So beautiful and so mesmerizing.

He was so different. Unlike everyone else I had ever met in my life. It was unusual, but at the same time so common that it confused my senses.

Chocolate brown hair and a sweet scent of his perfume. It drives me crazy. It was as perfect as the sun.
- Will you finally tell me what you want?
- I intend to offer you unforgettable memories. I intend to do my best to… -He put his thumb in my mouth and lifted my chin.

What do I do? He won't do it, will he? My God what do I do? I basically had him in my arms.
- Of all the tastiest sweets I've ever tasted, I'm sure you're the sweetest and at the same time bitter. -Did he just compare me to food?

It was beautiful...
He pulled me closer to him, pulling my head down and I didn't move or do anything. I closed my eyes, and it was what God and he, of course wanted. My heart beat a thousand times per minute. This was where I would have a heart attack.
Something warm landed on my forehead. Had he given me a kiss on the forehead???
If only on the forehead I was already like this, I don't even want to imagine what would have happened if he had kissed me on the lips.

Someone to save me.
- Become mine and I promise to give you a kiss properly. -I do...
- ...-I was speechless. That was very sudden.
- Did I exaggerate? Forgive me...
- No, it's okay, I'm just surprised by the request...
- Should we go. -Dark had appeared and interrupted. Thanks.
- I need you to tell me first because Lux knows you. - he asked Dark.
-Past memories. It doesn't matter. We need to go. It will be dark soon.

- Dark and I knew each other long before you were handed over to Pandora. It was long before God created the world where your brothers now live and the rest of humanity that also succumbed to chaos. -revealed Lux.
- How so?
- Soon after the evils took shape, God created the parallel world, Timeless, the gateway to the other side. The upper world, Prime, for beings who chose to follow the light and the underworld, Endless, the place where five children of Pandora are.
- What does this have to do with Gluttony and Dark? - I asked, still with him in my arms.
- Dark had once lived beside God but left heaven as soon as we realized his intentions. He lived on earth for millennia until he found someone to fulfill such evil desires. That's when Zeus destroyed God's creation. Endless or Pandora, the place where only the worst of evils meet. For humans it's a legend, but it's not. After opening the door in The Perfect City, the seven children decided to leave Olympus and live in Timeless. After that only five of Pandora's children, Pride, Greed, Wrath, Sloth and

Lust followed the path to Endless and the child behind that door, now Envy, had disappeared before the great gates had closed. Dark hid in this world, next to the one who had once been left behind, the one to whom indecision had accompanied his entire life. -impossible. It was surreal.
- Where is this Endless place? How do we get there?
- We don't. -I still found it hard to believe, but inside me there was a part that felt such an existence. - Endless as I said is in the underworld. To get there you need to get to Timeless first.
- Where is Timeless?
- Timeless does not have a specific place. It goes beyond the seas and oceans, beyond the mountains and plains… where dream and reality are one.
- So how do we get there?
- Only those who can hear the chimes can see their way there. Those who decide to become Walkers.
- How do we get them back? Can't you go in there?
- As Dark was forbidden to enter Prime I can't enter Endless.

I looked at Gluttony who was still in my arms, but who already looked better. I helped him up once more and stayed by his side just in case.

- No problem. I would never ask you to take that weight as your own.
- I know, but... No... -Something was approaching me.
It wasn't time yet; the sun was on the horizon, and I saw the sky open. The universe was now before my eyes. The sounds of beautiful melodies danced in the air and the chimes began to sound.
I closed my eyes, and my soul was filled with magic.
- What's it?
- I feel something calling me. I can hear beautiful melodies and the ringing of bells.
- See anything? -Lux asked me.
- I see the Universe. It's so close I feel like I can touch it. -I stretched my arm towards the sky.
- I never thought it would arrive so fast, but it did, and I won't be able to stop you from leaving if that's your decision.
- I don't understand.

- What you hear is Timeless opening the doors for you. The Universe is calling you.
- But I don't see anything. How will I know where to go or if I'm already there?
- You will know. You need to go before the last toll sounds. If this is what you chose then you need to go now. -how would I go there? I know I said I would help Gula, but how? It was all so surreal and hard to believe...
- Army? -Gluttony called me.
- What did you call me?
- Army. Isn't that your name?
- Yeah, but it's the first time you've called by name.
- Don't you like it? -I loved.
- I liked it. -I smiled and for the first time I saw him smile. His smile was beautiful. Gorgeous to die and hurt.

- Army?
- Say it.
- You don't have rondo this.
- I know that. I want to do it. For me too.
- I never thought all this pain would ever go away.
- It disappeared?
- Not completely, but whenever you're with me it's like she was just imagination.
- You changed my life too. Even though I met you a short time ago, I feel like I've known you forever.
- I feel the same way. -that was like a farewell, I didn't know where I was going, or if I would ever return.

My eyes were fixed on his and as much as I wanted to go, I wanted to stay here forever. It was crazy, but I felt my place was here. By his side.

- Are you still in pain?
- Not anymore.
- If you feel it, let me know.
- You won't be here if she comes back.
- That's true.

- I will just think of you and it will soon disappear. I am sure.
- What beautiful words.
- Beautiful is what you are and you're doing for me. It is beautiful to know that you will be mine when you return and that no one will be able to change you. -Beautiful. My heart can't stand so many beautiful words.
- More beautiful are you. Beautiful as the sunset. Beautiful as a full moon.
- Become mine. I will make you my only favorite flavor. The only flavor I'll get addicted to. -his hands were on my face and our bodies glued to each other. My strength was out of my body. What do I do? What do I say?
- .... - I wanted to talk, but nothing came out of my mouth...
- Sorry to interrupt, but you need to go. They are all waiting for you. -thanks. Gluttony smiled but continued to look at me.
- She's going. -he replied smiling. - You were saved... For now. - warned.
- You need to be careful with the princes.
- They're his brothers, they shouldn't be dangerous. Right?
- They may have human bodies, but they're like gods. They are the absolute law of that place. -I looked at Gluttony.
- Don't worry, I'll be fine. -he said.
- I will return with them. Promise. – I said to him smiling.
- Thanks. Beware.
- I'll will?
- You must have. Watch out for all of them, but the most powerful of all is Superb, also the oldest in transformation.
- Thanks for the advice. -I was already scared.
- You better go before it closes.
- Is better. -I walked, but then I stopped and looked at him. - Who is Dark? I feel like I know him, but I've never seen him before. It was the same to you, whenever I talked to you, but I already know who you are...
- Army? -Gluttony called me before heading towards the sunset. – Come back to me.
- I'll be back. -I smiled and there I went.

Greediness#

After that door had been opened, they all left. They all went their own way. After that, everything around him had changed.
I never thought hearing that sound would make me so happy. This time it opened, and it wasn't for me. Even though I knew that I will never turn back time, I now knew that a new future would come, and this time it would come for all of us.

From now on I will be prepared for their coming and I will know that they will be walking towards me every time I hear the gates open.

"I wasn't, I was never the most perfect man in the world, but for her I would try to be."

I had picked up her camera and placed it in position. I wanted to register that moment. Wanted to register Army heading into the sunset, as we once went also.
All lined up together. It was like before; it was like the day when the youngest opened the door and told him with his hand outstretched:

- "...The cruel world you lived in has ended and a new one awaits your arrival..." - He just looked at us without understanding. They headed towards the sunset, almost as one... And I was left behind, because of my indecision.
How much nostalgia did this memory cause!?

I had lowered the camera, because I knew that it was no longer necessary to keep that memory, because even seeing them go away, I now had hope.
Now I had a dream... The dream I had once lost in the beginning. The dream that one day I would meet them again and that this time I would walk beside them, together with Army.
Now I knew it was possible. My regret now turned into just longing, longing for those I had once let go.

HOPELESS

(I didn't know what would happen after I freed that poor soul, but I thought I was doing good until I opened it. Then it was too late for all of us. I didn't know, but I reached out to evil, and we were all dragged with it to Eternity.)

Army

I got rid of everything I had and entered that world naked and virgin of emotions and feelings.
It was dark, it was very cold, a dark, creepy air had passed over me and dragged me with it.
Just in the distance there was a small spot of light. I ran towards it and...

I opened my eyes and noticed I was in a strange place. The ceiling was light, it had a beautiful diamond lamp attached to it. It was like stars at sunset. Strange, isn't it? It was nostalgic. I could feel that I belonged here.

I got up and noticed I was barefoot. I walked to the door and opened it. A huge noise invaded my ears overwhelmingly.

I walked down that huge hallway and entered a room. The only one that didn't have a door, but two burgundy curtains that separated us.
That's where the noise came from... The music.

I pushed them away and came face to face with a kind of gentlemen's bar....
Was it a Host?
Well-dressed men and women drank and socialized with each other. Too few men and too many women to be frank.

Among them was someone, over in the left corner, who intrigued me. He wore a black shirt with sleeves rolled up to the elbows, a gold tie, black tuxedo pants, and black patent-leather formal shoes with a silver sole. A gold watch on his right wrist and rings on some of his long fingers on both hands. Well-groomed hair and an elegant look.
His striking presence had caught my attention.

He looked at me... I couldn't make it out because someone had pulled me by the arm.
- You can't be here. Not dressed like that.
- I was just passing by...
- Are you sure? - He asked. That voice wasn't strange to me, but I couldn't see anything because of the mask.

We entered a room... in the room where I had woken up.
- Wear this and put it on. - It was an elegant outfit. Beautiful and very luxurious. Too much for me.
- I cannot. This outfit is not mine. Besides, I said I was just passing by. I don't even know how I got here...
- You're talking a lot and doing nothing. Wear this and put it on.

I went to the bathroom and changed. When I left, I saw him by the door with his hands behind his back.
- I knew it would be okay. Are you ready? But first...put this on.

He took his hands behind his back and showed me a mask.
- Why are you helping me stay? I thought you were going to kick me out of here...
- Do you want to leave? I thought you had something important to do.
- I have... How do you know...? Who are you? - He took off his mask and... - What are you doing here?
- I didn't stop asking myself the same thing.

- You don't know who you are?
- I Know. But now it's not important.
- Where are we then?
- Don't you feel?
- Endless? I didn't think it was possible to get here without going through Time... - He didn't let me finish, covering my mouth.
- Don't say that name. Nobody can know that you came from another world and what you came to do. And I also thought it wasn't possible, but with you I've seen that anything can happen.
- Why can't I say Time... that name?
- The laws here are banal and for now you only need to know two things. This is one of Lust's pleasure houses and never look him directly in the eye.
- Why?
- All of them are the so-called sons of Lust. And among them the worst of all. Lust itself.
- Wow. Put it that way it sounds scarier than it already is. What happened to whoever did this?
- Does not matter. Just do what I ask of you. Now we must go.
- Where?
- To the ball. It's the anniversary of Lust and one of the most dangerous days of the year.
- Why?
- You'll find out.

Lust#

It was a pleasant evening. The atmosphere was also pleasant. The midnight bell had just rung, and the day was ending. The sun and moon were side by side, ready to switch positions.

Standing, clutching the microphone, I sang with my eyes closed as I melted into a thousand emotions due to that intriguing melody.
- So much sadness in one melody. Why? -he asked me after I missed a note.
- I've felt a strange presence for some time now. -I replied, and I realized that that bothered him too.

- Felt it too. But don't worry, I'll see it. Now get ready for the ball, the main guests should be arriving.
- He will come.
- I don't know, but even if you do, don't be fooled by his presence when you see the court of Nycteus, I don't want to be disappointed when you realize he didn't come with them.
- Never showed up and I wonder why?
- Do not create false expectations. We must not wish for what we know it will not happen. Get ready, they are waiting for you.
- I'll go right away.

Army#

It was all very beautiful and luxurious. It all seemed too much for me, but I would have held my ground if he wasn't with me.
- What do I do...? - I couldn't talk to him because someone had pushed me. Suddenly, the music stopped, and everyone stopped doing what they were doing.
- Good. More this one now. - I looked for Lux, but I couldn't find him anywhere, or maybe I had seen him, but as they were all wearing masks I hadn't noticed.
I walked through the crowd and continued my searches.

Storyteller#

- His Highnesses, Prince Superb of Merope, King Avarice of Alcyone, Prince Wrath of Maia, Prince Sloth of Taygete, and lastly his Highness Prince Lust of Sterope.

All showed off their beauty and their custom-made costumes from unique fabrics. The first Superb, the most beautiful of muds, the prince of perfection, accompanied by his court who also had their faces covered with masks, wore a bright white tunic, giving the illusion of having been made with heavenly bushes, on top of a kind of robe of the softest silk that could be found in all the realms, indigo, eyes of the same color transporting them to a journey through the universe, white hair, silver slippers and in both hands golden rings showing their long ones and delicate fingers and without forgetting he held his mirror offered by his mother. Right after that his brother, Avarice, who wore black pants of the most expensive leather, a dark green shirt that matched his slightly light eyes, a crown with the most varied precious stones that could exist, displayed his grandiose title of king, a cloak over his shoulders in gold on top and silver on the inside, was dragged as he walked, gold-soled, well-varnished shoes, dark black hair, and a hand full of gold coins attested to how miserly he was... Not far away, Wrath followed the red carpets that matched the strands all over his unkempt black hair, gave him a wild look and red eyes, wore tight pants with several rips again in black, dark red shirt where he left the first four buttons unbuttoned, sleeves rolled up to the elbows, and he held his most favorite book, written by himself, varnished shoes trying to contain all the strength that overflowed in his steps. And last but not least Sloth, who unlike Wrath kept a light and barely audible step, guided by his bare feet, wore a suit that looked more like pajamas, in light blue color, and a long robe, which looked more like to be embraced by the universe itself, light violet hair and eyes of the same color, but darker, some feathers over his head, showed that he had just woken up, holding his most faithful friend made of the same feathers that had fangs in his hair. So was the eldest of Lust who in turn was standing in front of his throne, He wore pants in the same style as Avarice, blue shirt with the first three buttons unbuttoned, a gold watch with diamonds on his left wrist, shoes varnished, and gold soles gave him a luxurious look, dark blue hair and eyes the same color. Both ears with earrings, three small ones on the right and two small ones plus a long but not too big key-shaped one on the right. Was he the host of the ball.

Army continued to look for Lux but ended up tripping over her dress and staggering to the center, where the princes were passing.

She stopped and everyone looked at her, including the princes.
- Good. Worse is impossible, -she said to herself.

- You think? -Wrath asked, who was right in front of her.
- Perhaps.
- Still answer. - He laughed ironically. - Who are you? Why are you here? You belong to which kingdom?
- I could answer that, but...
- Do not answer. Just your voice irritates me. Now get out of my way or I'll have to step over you...
- Try if you think...- everyone was shocked and at that same moment Lux appeared and took her away.
- I apologize immensely, Your Highness. She regrets what happened.
- No I don't...
- Let's go. -Lux took her by the arm and pulled her away.

As Army passed them, each one felt something strange coming from her, but they said nothing.

Army#

Back in the room Lux released me and I removed my shoes and mask.
- But who does he think he is to talk to me like that...? - I almost screamed.
-He is the child of danger. What were you doing there?
- I was looking for you.
- My father... Can't you still stay away from them? Wrath is the most violent of all and believe me, you won't want to cross him again.
- I'm not afraid.
- But you should. Now you stay here and only leave when I come to get you.
- Where would I go?
- Got it, Army?
- Yes. I understand, sir.
- I'm serious. It's dangerous for you.
- All right. I'll stay here. Do not worry.
- See you soon. - He left and I changed my clothes.

Since I'm going to be busy saving lives and humanity, I decided to get some rest.

I was lying on my bed…better in the bed Lux had made for me, but for now it was mine. Thinking about everything that had happened. It was already night, and I was more than bored.

The party was already over and... Someone had knocked on the door.
- You can come in. -I said, but no one opened it. They knocked again and this time I got up and went to the door to see who it was. It couldn't be Lux, because if I knew him well, he wouldn't do that sort of thing.

I sighed and closed the door and as soon as I turned around, I almost went into cardiac arrest.
- What are you doing here...? But who are you after all? - I yelled.
- Prince of Lust, why? Are you going to talk to me like you talked to Wrath?
- Sorry. What are you doing here, your highness? - I asked and kept calm.
- You said I could come in.
- By the door. Do you want me to die?
- If it were Wrath in my place, yes, he would want this.
- Thanks for the comforting words.
- You're welcome, but I don't see anything comforting in them.
- Forget... Forget it.
- I forgot.
- What did you come here for? How did you find me?
- I came to meet the person who faced my brother.
- You already know who I am, so you can leave now.
- I came to get you.
- Excuse me?
- I have nothing to excuse you for. Get ready we're leaving. -I think someone here is controlling and lacking a sense of reality.
- No, we won't.
- Of course, we will and that's why I'm here. Do you have clothes?
- Possessive controller has nothing. I don't know you nor the prince me. You don't know anything about my life.
- So, tell me. Tell me about yourself.
- No.
- All right. As you wish. -he said, and went to the door and I sat down on the bed. - What are you doing?

- I'm sitting down.
- Why?
- Because yes and because I'm not leaving.
- How can you not?
- I said that I do not want and even if I did, I had nothing to wear that was up to you, your majesty. Not that I want to go anywhere with you... now, go away.
- I figured you'd say so, so I brought you something to match me. -He didn't say that.

But what part of "Not that I wanted to go anywhere with you" and "I'm not going" that he didn't understand?

I looked at the dress and shoes he placed on the bed and then at him.
- I'll be waiting for you in the room next to Lux. Don't overdo the delay. Madam.
- You're kidding right?
- Not at all.
- But what's your problem?
- None. I just like things to go as I plan them.
- Do not tell me? I still hadn't noticed. - I smiled ironically sighed.
- Hurry up.

After I left, I pulled the dress away from me. I lay down and closed my eyes. Who does he think he is? Just because he's a prince, does he think he can boss me around?

"Yes, Army. That's right."- Damned subcontinent.

As much as I didn't want to wear it, I couldn't look away. I had no other choice.
Ahhhh what a rage.

I got up and opened the plastic bag that protected it. How beautiful it was. It was princess-style magenta with a long train. High shoes, silver rose, I might as well wear a suit and tie, I wouldn't mind at all.
- Of course, I'm not going to dress you, but I'm sure it would be beautiful.

I showered and decided to wear it... just to see how I looked. It could be bad...
- I knew it would fit you perfectly. - How does he... regardless of what he says won't change the fact that I don't go, period.
- Can't you beat yourself? - I diverted the subject. - There is a word that people normally use called "privacy".
- Far be it from me to take away your privacy. It was taking so long, that I thought of all sorts of situations that could lead to a delay. - In addition to being obsessive, he is paranoid.

Handsome... Not him... too... Forget it.
- If I could let his highness die of boredom. - I said and I shouldn't have done it.
He, I don't even know how, but he came at a frightening speed through the room, grabbed me by the arm and threw me onto the bed, so that he was on top of me.

The fact that he was wearing a beautiful black tuxedo, classic shoes, the same color and varnished, a gold tie, white shirt, some gold daggers, and well-groomed hair, did not stop him from moving quickly.
- What did you say? -he asked and I just looked at his beautiful sinful eyes.

As they were beautiful, even though it was already dark, the color of their blue eyes could be clearly noticed. They looked like they sparkled like diamonds.
- I said if you could die of boredom. -again, I shouldn't have repeated it. Damn mouth.

He took both my wrists and pinned them above my head with just one hand.
- Do you want me to die? -He frowned.
- Apparently you don't know the meaning of the word irony. - I told him.

God, his face was so close to mine and my heart couldn't take so much temptation together.
- Let's say we're not exactly friends. Irony is treacherous and I don't like women who hang around with it.

- Is it like you too?
- You? - Made a suspicious face. He couldn't find out what I was doing in Endless. Lux would kill me if that happened.
- As your highness.
- Of course not.
- Can you let go of me?
- Do you want me? - Of course, I did.... I wanted to say no. Of course not.
- Sorry?
- Your eyes have landed on my lip's countless times. -he smiled. Damn you.
- No.
- You are a bad liar. It's the third time you bite your lip. You want me. -he smiled and laughed through his nose. A thousand damn times.
- Do you think you are the apple of sin, luxuriously tempting and sinful?
- I am luxuriously pleasurable and sinful. I use and abuse of my sin, without pity or pity. - Someone saves me. I think I'm slowly dying. The air is fleeing, and the heart can't take such daring anymore. Help.
- I could make you mine right now, but we'd keep the guests waiting. -Nothing pious. Where is my sanity when I need it most?

He released my wrists but remained in the same position. Wait... it was even closer.
- Get up if you don't want me. – Excuse me? You are playing with fire. How does he want me to get up?

I didn't do anything or say anything, but I thought of lots of things, lots of them... But I just kept looking at those beautiful eyes and lips.
- I knew you wanted me. - How can you be so annoying? He got up and walked to the door. - Come.
I'll kill him if you give me any more orders. Revolted I put on and... someone was taking my measurements.

I left the room and followed him to the room where Lux was.
- Beautiful as a flower just blooming. - He looked at me and smiled and I smiled back.
-*Traitor* -I told him.

Lust looked at him and made a serious face. We've only known each other for a short time, and you already think I belong to you. Keep dreaming.

Storyteller#

Lust took Army to the city. They entered a private restaurant, but with a few guests, perhaps the ones he had invited, but at separate tables. He looked at them and greeted them with a nod and they went to their destination. Luxury landed in every corner of that space. In the corner of the room a red curtain separated another space, a huge room, with some tables spread out and one in the center, set for them. A bar at the end next to the exit door.
Army was watched by the women there, both accompanied and employed, as she walked beside him. Lust was a gentleman and pulled out her chair, inviting her to sit down.

Army#

All this for me was like living a fairy tale. Could I be happier than this? I could, I was, I just thought it was an exaggeration. I looked at him and he had his face turned to the side. I followed his gaze and there was someone, a beautiful woman like everyone else there. They kept exchanging glances and nods. She smiled at him even though she was accompanied by a man. I looked around and they were all looking at our table, as this sin in person made a point of reserving it on purpose.

- Good night. - said a maid, looking at him and then noticing that I was sitting there too. - I was told to deliver this to you. -she told him and handed him a red handkerchief along with a black envelope and left.

Lust opened the envelope and smiled... At least he could hide it.

He looked to his left side and by the bar was a woman, long black hair, wearing a dark red dress and black stilettos. She was drinking a glass of whiskey on ice and beckoning him.

The food hasn't even been served yet and you're already looking for dessert...? I know... It was too soon.
I feel like I'm going to kill someone...
It wasn't jealousy, but something was building inside me that was becoming impossible to bear. I got up and left the restaurant not caring if he was staying or not.

Storyteller#

After Army got up from the table, Lust didn't think twice, put down his handkerchief and envelope and rose towards the bar. The woman who was there was hopeful and walked towards him, but he bowed and went towards the exit.
- Where do you think you're going? -he asked, holding her arm, after having almost run after her.
- Far away from here... Why? Did you bring me here just to show me how much you are wanted? I already saw it. I'm not like these women; I'll never measure up to you and I'll never want to be.
- That doesn't interest me.
- Regardless of all the luxury I have, I will never be compared to them. I don't need this for anything.
- Tell me what you need, and I'll give it to you.
- What I want you can't give me.
-Say it.
- I just want to forget.
- What?
- All this.
- Do you want to forget me? -he asked disappointed with her answer.
- .... -I did not answer.
- Already understood.
- I didn't say yes.

- You didn't say no either. Your silence for me meant yes.
- No, I do not want. I just want you to understand...-she said, but he didn't want to know.
- Let's go.
- Where?
- Let's go back. -he said, turning his back on her and walking back to the house.
- ...- she wanted to say something, but he wouldn't respond, much less listen to her.

Army#

What a night, as soon as we arrived, everyone went to his side. I lay down on the bed and closed my eyes. I intended to forget everything that had happened and wake up the next day and it was all just a dream.

Storyteller#

It was morning the next day and Lust was still in the room. On the other hand, Army was with Lux, in the palace kitchen.
- I still don't understand what made him change his mind. I thought he were going to kick me out of here.
- Just knowing me helps. Also, because I told the prince you were my niece.
- OH, thank you so much uncle. -she hugged him and gave him a kiss on the face.
- You're welcome, niece.
- But you won't get in trouble for lying? On top of it, to a prince?
- Don't worry about it. What are you going to do now?
- I don't know yet, but maybe I'll go out for a walk.
- Don't stray too far from the palace, don't delay.
- Yes sir. See you soon... Uncle. -She smiled and left the kitchen.

While Lux was talking to some servants, still inside the huge kitchen, about his "niece", he hadn't felt that there was someone watching him from afar.

Army#

The prince was still in the room, from what I heard he would be ill.
Not that I'm worried. But it's hard to imagine someone like him getting sick.
I walked through the huge corridors while looking at the moldings that graced the entire wall. Large, medium, and small, doors and furniture gave a luxurious and very sophisticated air to the hallway.

A strange aura approached me lightly and hugged me tightly, causing shivers all over my body.
- Lady? Looking for something? - someone touched me on the shoulder, and I got scared.
-... -I looked back and saw that it was one of the employees. I was so scared the words wouldn't come out.
- I'm very sorry. -he walked away and bowed. - I didn't mean to scare you. - he said still bent over.
- Don't do that, don't even call me "lady". Call me Army. Only Army. - He straightened up.
- But his highness...
- He did that? - Bastard. - But who does he think he is? Now he decides who should call me by name or not? - Damn you. - Where is his room?
- Upstairs, but... - I didn't hear what he had to say, I let him talk to himself and went upstairs.

I went up that huge staircase... My God, this never ended... but finally I was on the second-floor and... I sat on the last step to rest...
- Why are you here? - Holy Father. But can you stop scaring me?

I got up quickly, and when I turned around, I saw him. I don't know how, but I barely stepped on the step and slipped. I expected to feel some pain, but nothing.

I slowly opened my eyes and there he was again, accompanied by the same strange, hopeless feeling. I looked deep into his eyes and felt lost, felt nothing. So empty and haunting that it sent goose bumps up my spine.
- Thanks. - I straightened and walked away from him.

I had never met anyone like him... That's what I thought.
- It's a pleasure to see you again. - How could something like that be possible?

Storyteller#

Army was still staring at the person who had saved her on that staircase.
- How...? I thought that...
- What did you think?
- Impossible, it can't be him. -I whispered.
- I don't know who you're confusing me with, but I'm sure we've never met before. I would remember if that had happened. - She looked at him, still suspicious, but soon composed herself.
- You're right. Maybe I messed up. I apologize.
- If you're looking for the prince, I'll let you know that he's not there. -he said after Army had passed him towards Lust's room.
- Do you know where he is then?
- I don't know, but even if I did, I wouldn't tell you, because his majesty doesn't want to see you. Also, don't be fooled, because Prince Lust doesn't attach itself to anything or anyone, much less a simple girl like you.
- I don't want anything from him. - They turned to each other.
- Then get out of here. Just leave and never comes back. I'm sure you won't miss him nor he will miss you.
- Who do you think you are to tell me what to do?
- Someone who will have no problem eliminating any problem or obstacle that comes my way.

- I'm not afraid of you.
- But you should. Now get out of here and never come back. He has his ladies to give him what he needs, you don't need to stay.

Army didn't say anything, just walked past him and down the stairs and towards the exit of the palace.
She had left, never to return.

Lust had just left the room and "he" was still in the same place.

- What are you doing standing here? - he asked as he approached him.
- Nothing. And your highness, what are you doing outside the room? Are you already in a better mood? Want something?
- So many questions... It's a yes to all of them.
- I see so. So, what do you need me to do?
- I need you to prepare the private room. Tomorrow I will receive visitors and we will have lunch there.
- For how many people?
- Five.
- As you wish. Do you have any preferences for the menu?
- Ask Lux to cook.
- So, I will. What do you want for lunch today?
- Nothing. I'm not having lunch here. - Lust descended, but then stopped. - Dark? Did you happen to see Lux's niece?
- The girl you took out last night. - He asked.
- Didn't you have another question?
- I had, but...
- Not interested, but herself. Did you see her or not?
- No, I didn't see her...
- Your Majesty...? -called one of the employees who was looking for him desperately, but as soon as she found him with Dark, she was silent.
- What happened? Why such a hurry? - He asked. - You can go Dark! -he told him.

After Dark left, Lust talked to his employee and after that each went to their side.

Army#

But who does he think I am after all...?
I still found it hard to believe that he was so much like Dark. Impossible, it could only be impossible, as he himself had said. That's right, it was impossible.
I don't know where I was, but I wouldn't go back either, or even if I tried, I would end up losing even more.
How huge it was and everything very luxurious. It is in fact the most luxurious and sophisticated city I have ever seen and been to.
It was nearly noon, and I was sure Lux was looking for me. My dear "uncle".

I walked back and passed a store, where there was a huge variety of sweets. Everything was so beautiful that it was even a pity to see people eating them.
- How is he now? - I thought aloud. I wondered about Gluttony. What would he be doing now? I don't know...but he'd probably be eating as usual. I smiled just remembering...
Maybe, but he was different. He had changed before I came here. He now thought differently, now he trusted me, but I just wasn't sure if he would keep his promise.

It was all so complicated. It all felt so right and impossible to change, even if it was a stone of the place, let alone Lust's way of thinking.
He was impossible to put up with and the fact that he thinks he's my boss or that I'm like all the others here, makes me want to kill him and... Let's think about good and beautiful things.
I continued my way and felt more and more lost.
I entered what looked like a small park, but I was wrong, it was a giant forest.

The Moon was already appearing, and time seemed to stop for a moment. Maybe it wasn't just an impression and it had really stopped...
- Someone looks lost. - But...? Could it be that this one doesn't know how to keep his distance?

- Why are you here? How did he find me?
- I'm asking the questions here. -compulsive abused.
- You can do whatever you want, I won't answer any. -I tried to pass by him, but he held my arm preventing me from going anywhere.
- First, why did you leave the palace without telling me? - Doesn't he hear? - Second, why did you give the employees permission to address you by name? And third, why do you treat me as if I were a simple ornament? -excuse me? In my world this is called ignoring.
- ...- I did not answer. I was, but I didn't.
- I asked three questions and I'm waiting for three answers.
- I don't think so.
- Do not play with me. You owe me obedience; I am your prince.
- You're not. You are nothing to me. But since you're so insistent, I'll give you the three answers you want so badly, I just can't guarantee they're the ones you want to hear.
- That... - he was going to say but I didn't let him finish.
- First, I don't have to warn you about anything. I came away never to return. It's definitive.
- Sorry?
- Sorry not sorry. Second, I'm not yours to decide who should call me by name or not. The name is mine, not yours.
- But...
- Silence, I'm not done yet. – he frowned.
- Third, I'm nothing to you. You are nothing to me, so I don't understand why you care so much about what I do? No life? You don't need me for anything...
- Can you...
- You never needed; you always had your ladies to give him everything you wanted...
- It wasn't that...
- I understood perfectly, you don't need to justify yourself. I'm me, I don't belong here, I don't even know why I came. I don't know you, nor do you know me...
- Again...
- He was right...
- He who...?

- You won't change, nor will it ever change and I... I thought... - I said without stopping, but... the words didn't want to come out this time. I think they ran out.
- What did you think? He who? Why would I change?
- See? That's why I find it impossible.
- Change me? - I looked away. - Why would I change what I am? - he shouted.
- Because there's more than this out there. There's more to it than Endless.
- You...
- I'm not from here. I came from there. There are things like these, but different, completely different.
- How did you get here?
- I do not know.
- Who sent you?
- Nobody.
- LIES. Are you still capable of lying to me after all? - he continued to scream. - I took you to my house. I trusted you and you lied to me...
- You never asked. Also, if I had told you who I am, you would never let me stay...
- Did you try? I always asked you to tell me about you, you were the one who didn't want it... -he stopped and sighed. – I would have let you stay if you had told me the truth. - he said calmly.
- Would you? Wouldn't you have arrested me and thought I'd be a spy from another realm or something worse? Wouldn't you have condemned me or something?
-.... - did not answer.
- As I thought.
- Perhaps it had been otherwise.
- How so? Crueler? I'm from another world... I don't belong here, nor will I. No matter how long I stay here or how much I must change to look like this... I'll always know this isn't my world.
- But I feel so... Since the day of the ball, I felt like I knew you forever. I can't explain it, but it's like I already knew you...
- Even if it does, nothing changes, it only gets worse for me. Now that you know who I am.
- Nothing will happen to you.

- Why not? Why do you insist that nothing will change if I come back?
- Because I'm the prince of this kingdom. My words are laws...
- I'm not yours.
- Why not?
- Impossible to talk to you.
- Come back with me.
- I thought you were going to kick me out.
- Why?
- Last night didn't go like...
- Already understood. I intended to do it or maybe lock you in the dungeons until you learned to obey me... Or maybe it would go to trial for mistreatment me in public. One of them. - he spoke as if it were something normal, but I was also the one who asked.
- Wow. And even said it might be different if I had told the truth about being human. I believe it would be... Very much.
- Come back with me? - he insisted. He was looking at me for an answer. It would have to be what he was looking for.
- No. I left the palace not to return.
- Then do as you see fit.
- Will return? - I asked as soon as he turned his back, but he didn't answer me. - Not going to answer? Are you going to pretend you didn't hear me? - he pretended not to hear me and continued walking.

Lust#

He would never ask again. I continued my way back to the palace and left her talking to herself.
- I came here not knowing what to do. The only certainty I have is that there is someone on the other side who misses you. Someone who once, in the past, shared dreams with you. -I stopped walking. Something inside me felt the truth in those words. - You know he would never blame you for what happened... To any of you. He just wants you back.
- You, who? You talk as if you know everything about me. - I turned around irritated and she was already very close.

- You. The princes of this world. They lost one of you. Gluttony, the eldest of Pandora's children. - how could she know such a thing.
- A human like you cannot know such a thing. Did you really come from the Human world and not from somewhere else? Have you come to destroy us?
- Already said no. I know Gluttony. I'm here for him.
- Why should I believe your words. Someone who's only lied to me so far can't show me the truth.
- I know you know what I say is true. Don't you feel it?
- What should I feel?
- The sound of something grand calling you? The sound of something new opening up for you. There's a lot more to the other side than just this. - I could hear. It was the same as last time. That was a long time ago.
- What else is there to satisfy me? I have everything here. I'm happy on this side.
- Are you? Don't you miss what you left behind? After that day?
- Maybe... Whenever I look into your eyes, I feel that everything you say is real, but after I think about them, everything seems so vague. Simple illusions.
- They are not.
- Then I'll only moderate if you stay with me. -I replied, but I wasn't sure it would happen.

Army#

Clever. How can a prince like him bribe someone like me?
- I'm not your luxury. I can't give you what...- He came closer and hugged me tightly. Something strange is happening.
- You are my dignity and I want you to make me worthy of you. -he whispered. - I want to belong to you forever. I want you to save me. I want to stay by your side forever. Changning who I am is the price to pay to have you with me, I will pay it. -so dramatic.
- I don't want you to change I just want you to become your true self...

The bell was ringing, it was like the sky was singing for us.
- Looks like time has stopped.
- The heavens are on our side. I could stay here forever with you. -he said.
- No.
- Everything is fine. So, what do I need to do to go to this place you talk so much about?
- You already know how. Follow the path you took when you came.
- Come with me.
- I cannot. I need to go save the ones that are missing.
- Will you be all right?
- I don't know, but I don't think so.
- Will I see you again?
- For sure. Do not forget, before the last chime sounds you must cross the great Gates of Wisdom and you will reach Timeless. Gluttony will be waiting for you. Promise that whatever happens you will cross them.
- Promise.

The light was so intense that I couldn't see it and I felt happiness well up inside me.

- I'm sure I'll know if you're still you, after looking deep into your heart. -He was. He entered that path without looking back. Now it was my turn to go, but where?

Lust#

The path was the same. I saw it all over again in my memory before that day arrived.
I saw the black door on that side of town, and it was overflowing with overwhelming force, but I had no idea what might be on the other side until I opened it and saw him at such performances.
He was looking at us persistently. That's when I reached out my hand and told him:

- The cruel world you lived in has ended and another awaits your arrival. -He smiled and squeezed my hand tightly.
It was then that I decided to look back...

(For those who once lost their shadow, I say that however much they both walk along parallel lines they will one day intersect, just as the sun and moon will meet at dusk and dawn.)

SLEEPLESS

(Sleep is a nocturnal melody that rocks life in a gentle but dangerous way… It wasn't because of lack of sleep that I didn't sleep, but because those memories never left my thoughts.)

Army#

I tried my best so none of that would change me. My willpower was big enough to share for them, but theirs need to be bigger to keep it strong.

Sloth#

I was already tired even without having to do anything tiring. You were the one who left me most tired.

We could have continued with this, I could have let you stay, but we both knew it… We knew we'd only get hurt even more…

The day was over, and night had arrived shortly thereafter. The moon was brighter than ever. Full moon. Beautiful, bright, and eye-catching. It was the first time he had appeared after so long away.

Why now?

I walked through the corridors of that place. After so many doors opened, they were closed today. There was something calling me. Like the last few times I tried to avoid him. I ran and the farther I ran in the opposite direction to that door, the closer it seemed to be.

I stopped right in front of it. Giving up running I touched the doorknob, but soon fear gripped me. It was back… Fate. The New Moon. The person I had driven away because of my fear. The person I avoided hurting, but the person I hurt the most. It was all back.

I took a step back and it opened… Fate had come against me, but I got out of its way before we collided with each other…

The road was still empty, but the whistles were still heard. After so long I still hadn't found the person behind them. That beautiful melody started to play, and I felt inside a dream that became a nightmare. I entered. I didn't know why, but I walked in and the ground under my feet turned cold. I had no shoes, and my clothes had changed completely.

A path of stones and water formed a small stream, the green grass gave it a light air, but everything looked so bleak. I was dizzy, I felt poisoned and tired, but I kept walking in a daze and… There was a bed full of pillows on a small island.

As soon as I put my foot in the water, it was as if the whole thing had abducted me.

Army#

I heard someone whistle a beautiful melody. It was so flashy, so powerful, it made me shiver. In the background I saw a beautiful "Flower of Phenix" on the ground and everything was taken by smoke.

I ran and continued running towards the exit, only to find a black door and something undecipherable desired in it. I got closer to her and as soon as I went to touch her, she opened.

Storyteller#

Army slept in the bed Sloth had found in his dream, but he was in front of the strange door he had found earlier.

Sloth opened the door wider and came face to face with Army lying on the bed. So innocent, so angelic that nostalgic feelings came to his heart. The ones he had fled from in the past.

Without thinking twice, he hurried up and dragged her out of bed and out of the room.

- Get out of here before I order you to annihilate. Now. Don't come back - he shouted at her and then closed the door.

Army was scared and not understanding what had just happened, but still, she went without saying anything. The moon was full and bright. Army left that house and sat down on the entrance steps.

- But what does he think he's doing or who does he think he is...? Have me annihilated? He's lost her mind. -she could only complain.

Army got up and walked towards the city, but first she stopped and looked back. There was something that called to her. A feeling of being watched and she was not wrong. In one of the windows Sloth watched her without any intention of hiding.

Both were hypnotized. That strange sensation and feelings he felt, the full moon, everything had a reason, and he knew that her appearance was related to everything.

After a few seconds Army turned her back and continued her way, but Sloth remained in the same place.

Army#

I walked and continued to walk, once again that feeling of being watched.

- Looking for something? - someone asked after touching my shoulder
- Lux? What a fright.
- What a fright I say. It's hard to find you. What happened?
- Nothing.
- You didn't convince me. Why that face? - I did everything for him not to see me cry.
- Nothing. It was hard to understand Lust... Only that.
- I get it. What are you doing out here alone?
- I was almost kicked out of a house, where I woke up.
- Why?
- That, too, I would like to know. I swear the next time I see him he'll listen and it's well.
- Keep the...
- I'm calm. Very calm. Let's go and look for that prince.
- All right. Let's get to it. – I followed Lux through the streets of that place.
- What's this place called? I know this is Endless, that's all.
- We're in Pleyades. It's... let's say the name of the planet.
- I don't understand.
- Good. For humans this place is the underworld, but for those who live here, the human world is the underworld. Do you understand?
- A bit.
- Continuing. This underworld the humans call it Endless, but what they don't know is that this is much more than a legend. We are in another dimension. Here, we have, Pleyades, in the human world Is a constellation, but after God created this place.
- I understand now.... I guess.

- Continuing, due to the changes in the universe all the stars collided and transformed into a planet and created realms, they are eight kingdoms, “countries” shall we say. Each of these realms has a king or prince.
- Like Lust.
- Exactly. Sterope, capital Oenomaus. Taygete, capital Lacedaemon. The only realm that has two capitals, Nyctea and Lycos from Celaeno. Maia, capital Hermes, Alcyone, capital Hyrieus and Merope the capital is Glauco.
- Already understood. I bet my world is like a legend to them.
- But shouldn’t there be seven kingdoms?
- Yes, and they are. Dardano capital of Electra. It’s like a ghost realm.
- Sounds like a fairy tale.
- But it is not. It’s pure reality.

Just seeing it, to believe it. Here those who crossed, are those who were condemned or exiled.

- Where are you going?
- To Timeless. Perhaps they can return into human.
- I call it a salvation.
- Two completely opposite realities. You are subject to condemnation. There is your reality, the one that only you believe in and this reality, the one that everyone else believes and defends.
- Lust believed me. They too can believe, maybe change their way of thinking.
- These people no longer believe in the other world. That’s why they’re still here.
- Because no one bothered to tell them. I’m here because Gluttony has decided to stay and wants his friends back.
- Friends, not the world below. Gluttony didn’t come because he was afraid and when he made up his mind it was too late for him and for the others.
- It’s not too late now. They respect their princes, don’t they?
- They have much more than just respect for their princes. Being you from another world, you should know better than everyone else. I’m sure you feel that. Even the people here feel it.
- What?

- You have a pure heart; you should be up there and not down here. Sooner or later, you will feel the temptation to want to stay and the weight these people carry... - was that what I was feeling? No.
- I won't. I have enough willpower to stay conscious and even if I feel that weight, I can bear it.
- Willpower may not be enough when the world is not in our favor. It's not like this.
- ... -I was going to answer him, but he spoke first.
- We're here. - he said, stopping in front of me.

Storyteller#

While Army was trying to understand what was happening and where they were, at the same time she was dazzled by it all, Sloth had gone out into the street to greet his old friend.

- Your Highness! - he bowed.
- Lux. What brings you here?
- I came to visit.
- You did well...- he replied and soon noticed that there was someone else with him.
- I almost forgot, my niece Army. Army? -he called her, and she went to him, but she stopped halfway after seeing Sloth.
- You?
- Me.
- Have you met?
- It was this person who ran with me almost on a kick. He even said he had me annihilated.
- I see.
- Are you?
- I thought I was very clear when I said not to come back. -he said calmly.
- I'm not leaving here until I finish what I came to do. Did you understand?
- Army, keep calm. I apologize profusely for my niece. I hope you can forgive her.
- As you wish. Come in... Just you, she stays.

Army#

I won't even say anything. It's Been a long time since he left with Lux.

I hope he knows where the prince is and that we can get out of this place as soon as possible. I walked through the garden, and it was all very beautiful, but it was all very nostalgic. I felt strange... I continued and continued walking until I reached a small garden. It looked more like a park. It had a small river, with stones forming a trail. I followed the water and it led me to a lake.

- Army!? Army!? - I heard someone whisper my name. – Come to me. Army!?

I wanted to go; It was stronger than me... And I did. I continued walking towards the water. I was close enough and... as soon as I touched the water everything was different.
The garden was gone, the space was different, totally different. It felt like a dream.

Storyteller#

Lux was still with Sloth.

- Who is that girl?
- Army.
- That's not what I want to know. Why did you bring her?
- She was with me in Asterope.
- In the palace of Lust?
- Exactly.
- Wasn't her the one who answered back to Wrath?
- You remember?
- It's impossible to forget.
- He just let her stay because she is my niece.
- Your niece? Since when do you have nieces?

- Since Army was born.
- When was that?
- It was...- he tried to answer, but the face that Sloth had made him worried. – What is it?
- Nothing. I just felt too hot inside.
- In fact, it's strange because it's a bit cold in here.
- It's the moon.
- What about it?
- Her too.
- Who?
- Army. –he said and then dropped to his knees.
- Sloth?
- Burn...

Army#

I felt my heart become more intense and....

-Army. Army -I heard it again.

Something shiny caught my attention deep inside. I walked closer and noticed that it was a burning lotus flower. Better saying the famous Phoenix Flower. I knelt to touch it, and everything was engulfed in smoke.

Sloth#

I dove headfirst into the water and my soul was taken by fire...

How deep this abyss was. So deep that not even it had ever seen its own end. My feet were exposed, barefoot. They stepped on the ground covered with icy water that scratched them as they tried to hold me, inviting me to sink into it. It was so tempting, so much more liberating than my current living condition.

I wasn't ready, that I couldn't deny. I wasn't ready for what was coming, for what she had brought back to me.

Army#

It was so dark here, so empty…too lonely for one person. Whoever was the soul that lived here would be at the limit of its condition.

I looked around and saw, far away in the distance, a bright spot. I didn't know what it was until I got close enough. A small round stone, but shiny. Soon after another and another. All I had to do was pick it up and soon everything was revealed.
A beautiful place like the garden where I had just been. I thought because that place bewildered even time.

A melody danced fiercely through the air. So evilly dark it made me shiver, it was so wonderful. It hurt my whole body, as if each note were a poisonous thorn. I barely moved. There he was once again, sitting at the piano. He was the owner of those magic fingers. So serene, but I could hear his soul scream for help.

Sloth was his name. The person I've been looking for all this time was right in front of me. So beautiful, so pitiful. Trying to reach him was like trying to cross a burning wall, but none of it was stronger than me. When I finally reached the piano, I noticed that little lotus flower, the same one I had tried to catch the last time before I came here.
Different from before, it was now almost completely black, withered and scarred by fire. So, I took it as carefully as possible, afraid it would break in my hands.

- I'll take yours and you take mine as if it had always belonged to you and don't let it go back to the dark, ever again.

(I saw life pass me by and nostalgia took hold of me instantly. So vivid, so full of memories as if they never left him. They were now also part of me.)

Storyteller#

Sloth had stopped playing and looked strangely at his little flower, beautiful and brighter than ever, until he saw Army standing looking at him with a smile on the face.

- What did you do…? - shouted. Army staggered and Sloth didn't let her touch the ground. - What did you do? She asked after the smoke had crept up onto the floor and the flames soon after.

Still with her in his arms, Sloth tried to get past them, but they were too strong and fell with Army.

Sloth#

I was dead. I had been taken by them again. I felt the ground under my body, and it was cold and wet. I opened my eyes one by one and looked for her. I looked everywhere, but it wasn't. I got up with difficulty and saw another piano not far from me. I heard a melody right away, the one I used to play in distant times.

- What do you want from me? -I yelled and covered my ears. I staggered and continued to stagger until I thought I had finally stopped.

I continued to look for her, even though I knew I would never see her again.

As I walked, the ground took shape and a lawn appeared in its place, soon after a blue sky and some gray clouds. There was no sun, no heat, it was like a spring day that you could only imagine what it would be like.

A cliff ahead invited me to look, so I went out knowing it would be a one-way trip.

Army#

(One day I wanted to play for those who could understand the meaning of each note. So, I closed my eyes and played, waiting for the wind to rise and carry them away. So that the lost could find their way back home.)

I didn't know where I was, but I was sure I would see him again. I continued to play and awaited his arrival.

- Even if you try to save him, you can never save yourself. -I heard.
- I don't believe those words. -I stopped playing, but the piano played alone.
- Here you are my son. I came to get you – it wasn't for me; it was for Sloth.

I turned around and there he was. Near that precipice.

- I'm here. - I yelled, and he looked back. – I didn't leave. I'm still here.
- I thought that...
- I didn't... I would never leave before I find you.
- I'm here. You can go. I don't need you to stay anymore. -he said and I saw a shadow on his right side.
- Don't listen to him.
- Why not? I've always listened to him, and I've always been fine, except now that you showed up. I'm here because you brought everything back.
- I didn't bring him; they came because you're finally ready to accept them.
- I don't want them back. I want to be able to close my eyes and rest. I want to stop walking without stopping.
- You can do all that, but for that you'd have to go back along the path you're so avoiding.
- I don't need to stop by to rest. He knows how to do it.
- You just dig deeper into those nightmares. You can trust me.
- Your words are like poisonous melodies.
- All right. I won't do it anymore but come back. I admit I'm to blame for your sleepwalking... I've got what you're looking for. -there was no other way. I had to save him even if he didn't want my salvation.

Sloth approached me slowly until he was face to face with me.

- Where is it?
- Over there. -I pointed to the piano. – Play and your sleep will return to you – he went and sat down at the piano. He looked at me and then closed his eyes. He played one and two notes. So beautifully that the melody seemed to come to life.

I walked towards the cliff and from there I saw it transform into something grand. He opened his eyes and saw me far away. On top of the piano something shiny was taking shape. That's when he realized what was to come.

- I asked you to stay away. – he shouted
- But you wanted the opposite. I heard you scream for me.
- You couldn't…
- I had no choice.
- Why me?
- At the beginning I didn't know it was you, but now you can move on without having to run.
- But go where?
- Find your light, your sleep.
- I don't have any of that anymore.
- You let them go.
- And you?
- Me? I have enough… Sloth… -I called him when he got close enough.
- Don't do it…-he despaired.
- Go. Now you can go, but first take her and protect her like the one you once let die. -I went to him and closed his hands and then opened them.
- Where?
- You will know as soon as you hear a mysterious melody, you will follow each note and before the last chime sounds for midnight, go through the Gates of Wisdom. He will be there waiting for you.
- Where?
- In Timeless. -I said and an echo made the word fly everywhere.

Storyteller#

Army was suspended in the air and before Sloth could reach her, she had crumbled to ash and evaporated into thin air.

- Army? - he shouted.

Sloth#

(The fact that I still haven't found the right path
for my journey didn't meant I was lost.)

So, I took my new soul carefully and everything took its true form. The silence was silent, but it screamed and whistled beautifully, haunting, and malevolent melodies. I was once just someone with as many imperfections as perfections and talents. I had been here before, but I didn't know where to go, or maybe I did, and I was afraid of what I might find later.

Where will she be now? The most strangely peculiar person I had ever met. I felt that I had known her forever. Strange, isn't it?

I didn't know what time it was, but it didn't last long before I heard the bells ring. A light ran towards me and hit me hard. My road had appeared, and the sound of a horn had me pulling away before I was hit by it.

- Sloth… -my name danced in the air. It was her voice. Impossible not to recognize her.

Now I knew what to do.

Trumpets were blowing high above, it felt like the sky was opening for me, but it was the gates that called to me. There were already two chimes there and I was still standing. So, I ran, and I ran even faster, until I finally saw the gates in front of me. So bright on the other side, so flashy…
A shadow appeared at the door, and I stopped.

- Army? Are you? - I was hoping it was her, but it wasn't, and that shadow was very familiar to me, even too much.
- Come. –that voice. It couldn't be him…
- You? How?
- We do not have time. Come with me… My brother. –it was him, yes.

Now there were only three chimes left. He held out his hand and I smiled as I ran towards him.

Army#

So light, yet so heavy.
Wherever I was, it was welcoming but at the same time scary. A light touch of wind swept past me at almost unreachable speed, and I knew Sloth had finally found his way back to his light.

Sloth#

A bell was missing, and the gates began to close. I've never run so much since the day I tried to escape fate.

Even before the door closed completely, I had walked through the gates and only then did I look back.

All that was now past, a past that I would leave behind and move from now on, looking straight ahead. Stop looking for emergency exits so much and focus on always keeping my only door open. The one of sanity.

So, this was the famous place. Timeless, the forbidden place. It felt… It was… I don't know, but so much nostalgia made my whole body shiver.

The day here was so much more real and so much more alive than I had ever felt it. The same as the night as bright as the full moon that lit up the sky.

I had a flashback and it reminded me of the day our lives parted tragically. So painful was that memory that I let myself be overcome by pain, once again and unconsciously I screamed your beautiful name.

I had lost track of myself, and the bell announced at one in the afternoon.

(A single toll had caused the whole world to hear the skies open and the changing times heralded the coming of great storms for those who felt it in the morning winds.)

OTHER

*(I tried to fight to show you that you were not alone, I tried
to save you, but I ended up falling with you…
I saw the fire consume you, but it was too late
to save you from all this revolt…)*

#Lust

*(I already had a reason to go back, but if I went back, I would be betraying
life. You were my salvation, but I chose to walk away from you. I thought
I was protecting you from me, but I ended up dragging you with me.
Even though I was the same on the outside, inside I had died, and this
was the beginning of a new life. The life I would live by your side.)*

#Sloth

HEARTLESS

(I was the first of them, but no one had realized it. It wasn't my choice; they broke me up little by little... I knew that evil was coming to me, and I had no choice but to tear myself from the punished body I carried. Until that moment I was the only one who kept us sane, but soon I would live against it, and I would also surrender to something crueler than this punishment. I didn't regret it, after I got rid of that weight and they took me away, but I could still see their faces before the farewell. I also ripped his wings so he wouldn't fly and never find me. Today we each live in our own corner, but in the same place, feeling his presence I will never manifest myself.)

Army#

It was dark, I wanted to hear someone, see someone, but I saw nothing but the immense darkness that surrounded me.
I felt everything around me getting colder, the air heavier and it was getting harder to breathe. I tried to fight that invisible force, but it was much stronger than me. I felt that there was something in me that was disappearing.
- Save me. Save me - I heard and then a laugh echoed throughout that space. It seemed to dance as it floated.

Everything was dark, as if I had been blindfolded, but my feet were flat on the ground, at least it seemed to be the ground.
I ran without an exact direction. I didn't know where I was going, but still, I didn't give up, I didn't even stop.
A feeling of nostalgia came over me and gave me more strength to run, as if I wasn't the only one running.
I stopped, suddenly. A glare hit my eyes and I looked back. They came against me. The memories were red hot and ready for our collision. I looked ahead and noticed I was in a kind of tunnel where I was still on the road and the exit seemed unreachable. Red and blue lights danced along its length, indicating an exit.

I ran with my eyes closed and for some reason I liked it, because I had a smile on my face. I looked back, expecting to find someone, but no one was there.

I was pulled back hard and fell to the ground.
- What are you doing here? - Something or someone held my hand...

I had a chain attached to my left hand that was held by a figure in black. I couldn't see the face in all that darkness.
- I asked what you're doing... - He pulled the chain and came closer. He looked me in the eye and then froze.
- What are you still doing here...? - someone interrupted.

He was not a normal, unusual person. A very distinguished aura... it was familiar to me, but I didn't know from were.
- You here? What a surprise.
- Who are you?
- Me? Someone important.
- How would I know.
- You'll know in time. Now come on, we have a lot to talk about - he said and pulled the chain that held me.

I got up out of obligation and walked after him like a criminal. Maybe a convict.
- What do you think you're doing? - a voice came from behind me.

- This, I ask. What are you doing here? Does he know you're here?
- He doesn't boss me around.
- Poor child, he thinks he has some authority. Why do you think you're still alive?
- I'll take her.
- Do not you dare! - my Lord. What is up? I'm getting scared.

Whoever was behind me pulled me closer and covered my mouth.
- Don't move! -he whispered in my ear. - I won't hurt you. Do not worry.
- Do not you dare.
- Stay where you are. -he shouted, and I was startled.

I closed my eyes tightly and waited to feel something.
The silence was constant, I didn't hear anything, didn't feel anything, not even the weight that my wrists used to carry. So, I decided to open them, and that place was empty, just me and me. It was then that white light hit me, and I turned my face to the side with my eyes closed.

I woke up under a beautiful, charming voice.

I opened my eyes and came face to face with a roof, not of glass but of wood, I got up and sat down.
- He's waiting for you. Don't be late.
- I'll be there.

There was no bed under my body, just a small mattress that was a little uncomfortable.
- Have you woken up yet?
- Where am I?
- Somewhere. -he said and I could finally see his face. He sat up and fixed his gaze on something.

So well dressed, so beautiful, so pure as a child. It was like it was. An adult-looking child.
- Who are you? Do I know you? - He looked at me and smiled.
- You don't remember. -he looked down and began to play with his hands.

- Remember what? I had a weird dream... -I looked at my wrists and saw the marks.
- It doesn't matter what happened. -he got to me as fast as if he had run. He covered my wrists with his big and perfect hands.

A tear fell from my eye and trailed down my face, but he stopped its path with his thumb.
- Nothing can change what happened. I know you're not normal, and neither am I, but believe me when I tell you that everything will change.
- Who was he? What did he want from me? -He sat down again, but this time he sat opposite me. A serious face made my heart sink.
- Sentinels. He was one of the Sentinels who guard the palace and dungeons. It was the first time you saw one, right?
- Yes. And what were you doing there?
- Me? He was waiting for you. They told me you would arrive.
- Did you know they would be waiting for me?
- Yes. Are you all right?
- Yes, I am. And you? Are you fine? - I asked and he looked at me strangely.
- Me? Why?
- You look worried.
- Do not worry. I am fine. - He smiled and got up. - Where are you going? -he asked me after I got up right away.
- I do not want to be alone. Where are you going?
- The city...
- I can go? I don't want to stay here. Please. I promise I don't do anything. I'll be quiet. Without moving.
- If we're going out, it wouldn't be pleasant or convenient to stay quiet and not move, don't you think?
- Why? Does that mean I can go with you? -He sighed and then I saw a smile.
- I can't leave you here alone, can I?
- No, thank you. -I ran up to him and gave him a big hug. - Sorry, I'm so excited. -I broke the hug and looked away.
- No problem. Let's go?
- Let's go.

We left that little cabin... It was a cabin. Wow. It was small and beautiful. It had an old-fashioned look, but it was very pretty.

We walked for a while, but all the time he kept looking around and back to see if I was still there.
- I'm still here.
- Can you come forward? Just to stay longer...
- Sure. Don't worry. I understand - ran forward.

After a few minutes in the forest, we reached the best part. A kind of giant village. There was going to be a festival... Some fair. Colors and many different smells made me surrender to all those wonders.
- Where are we? -I looked back and saw him surrounded by people.
- Come to my stall. This year we have many varieties. The harvests were blessed thanks to you... - said a old woman.
- Do not say that. It was all thanks to your effort. -she smiled back.
- Everything is fine. -for a moment he looked happy, carefree, so I decided to take a walk around the fair.

I saw this, I tasted that, and it was very good. Deliciously tasty were the right words to describe it.
- Want to try? - asked a old man, after having caught me peeking at his stall.
- Which is?
- Eve's liquor.
- From whom?
- From Eve. Made from the fruit that grows in Zeus' orchard. Prove. Maybe it's good.
- I can't pay but thank you very much.
- No need to buy the bottle, taste it. I don't charge for tasting. I noticed that you didn't take your eyes off the bottle.
- Are you sure?
- Trust me. -he held out a small glass of liqueur and encouraged me to drink it. There was no way I could resist it, so I picked it up and took it. Was...

- Wow. - it was.... Hot and cold at the same time. So sweet and bitter... Strange was the word.
- What do you think?
- Is weird...
- Where have you been? I looked everywhere for you. - he almost shouted.
- Me...
- You should have waited for me. -he yelled and a few people stopped to watch.
- But...
- But what? You know it's not safe and yet...
- You were busy, you looked happy then...
- So what?
- Your Highness...
- Your Highness? Are you a prince?
- Wait.
- You're a prince. He is a prince. - a prince. - Why didn't you tell me? You could have told me... - OK... I'm feeling something.

He was saying something, but I wasn't listening to him. The colors mingled and people seemed to mold themselves. Another time travels?

Storyteller#

Army was weird and Johnno started to get worried.
- Are you unwell? -he asked, but she didn't answer.

There was something about her that was different. Eye color, hair color.
- What did you take? Has anyone seen her take something?
- Your Highness? She just tasted Eva's liquor. Just tasted a little, I insisted. I did not know that...
- You are a prince. -she repeated it and repeated it repeatedly.
- Forgive me. It was not my intention.
- Do not worry. I solve this.

As soon as Johnno approached her and touched her to hold her Army fainted.
There in the distance, somewhere in those tents, there was someone who watched them silently.

Johnno#

Every night I had the same dream... The same nightmare.
Back pain was constant, but more painful whenever it played at twelve.
Both the sun and the moon brought up my most terrifying nightmares.

I was in my house. In my room trying to close my eyes, but I didn't dare do it. I don't know why, but every time I thought about it, fear took hold of me. It was almost noon. I got up and went into the living room.
- Couldn't rest again? -he asked. The person I trusted the most.
- Father. -I said, and I greeted him. - No, once again I couldn't close my eyes. The bells are about to ring.
- Do not worry. One day you will be able to enjoy sleep.
- I look forward to the arrival of that day. How is she?
- Still with a fever. Did she take anything?
- Eve's liquor.
- Army took it. How come?
- It was a customer who gave it to prove it.
- Call him here.
- It is not necessary. I've already talked to him. It wasn't with intent. Besides, he wouldn't guess what effect it would have on Army.
- This type of liquor is not sold in the city.
- I know, but he's not from here either, but I've already asked some guards to search the city. Before we left, I felt a strange presence.
- How can he be in town? You could have been more careful… Looking for Army?
- Calculable.
- Did you go get her?
- I had no choice. The Sentinels had her prey. They were going to take her to Nycteus.

- Johnno, I told you not to cross the forest alone.
- I knows. Sorry, but...
- All right. It was stronger, I understand.
- Do you think she'll be okay?
- I don't know, but with Army everything is possible.
- Father?
- Yes, Johnno?
- The sky. - was by the living room window. The sky was changing color. The gray clouds reached the city in the blink of an eye.
- Army! -he said and ran away.

As soon as I got to the room, I found Army suspended in midair.
One... Two... Three... It was already noon, and the moon was already approaching the sun.

Storyteller#

Johnno felt the change along with Army and she was stronger than him. All the people had seen the sky turn black, it wasn't normal, it had only happened once and the second time, it meant a bad omen.

In Nycteus, who was happy was Dark. That bad omen for him meant the coming of good times.
- Your Grace, the human is in Lycos with the prince, and he is already with Lux too. -said one of the Sentinels as he entered the throne room.
- Damn you! -he yelled and hit the arm of the chair hard, which made everyone there startled.
- The human took the liquor from Eva.
- So that's why I feel so good.
- What will you do now?
- Bring her to me. I want her before they make her go back to normal... She won't be the same again, but with her everything happens.
- It's for now.
- For yesterday.
- What do we do with Johnno?

- Nothing. Just avoid bumping into Lux.
- Won't he be weak while the human doesn't recover?
- Even so, he is and will be stronger than you. Unless I convert her.
- Understood. - they left and went to Lycos to get Army.

Dark#

(It wasn't the amount of power that made me fearful,
but how far I would go for it and with it.)

This feeling and strength growing inside of me was like all the power I deserve was merging with me of its own accord. Even though I know she was born to maintain the cosmic balance, I will have to at all costs comply with Zeus' wishes and avoid being sealed.

Johnno#

(I tried to stop the coming of night, as well as parting with my own shadow, but I only managed to make my world darken further.)

So scary whenever night comes. So invasive, all this darkness...
This anger I feel only increases with each chime, the countdown to midnight. It's as if my own shadow touches me and tries to get inside me. Beautiful, poisonous words filled my ears and drowned my brain.
It was the devil. My other self. So familiar, so nostalgic. So amazing, but it was my other half... The one I disowned without any remorse.

Storyteller#

While Johnno tried to fight himself, the sentinels were already in the palace ready to take Army.
- There's no one here. - said one of them.

- Better yet, but don't let your guard down. Lux won't let us take her so easily.
- You must believe. I won't.
- Lux? Dark asked...
- I know well. My answer is no.
- You know you can't stop us. -he said.
- You are sure? -He took a step towards them.
- We didn't come to fight.
- So, what are you doing here? Did you thought you were going to take her without having to face me?
- No, but Johnno disobeyed and crossed the border. He could not.
- It was stronger than him.
- Now they'll have to bear the consequences...
- Are you threatening them? That's it? You understand the last person who threatened them was annihilated...
- Dark aroused Envy. Johnno or the human, the choice is yours.
- Damn you Dark. -he was angry, and this caused a terrifying fear to the Sentinels, because irritating Lux was the same as challenging Dark or even God himself.

Lux didn't move, he let them pass because he couldn't stop them if he wanted to save Johnno.

Storyteller#

Johnno was trapped in his own nightmare, in the palace and Army was now on his way to the other side of the kingdom, Nycteus.
- She's on her way, your Majesty.
- Where is he?
- In the palace. Do not worry. Lux won't cause any problems for a while.
- Fortunately. They didn't hurt the child, did they?
-Don't worry, she hasn't suffered a single scratch. Lux made a point of keeping us away.
- Did they find him?

- He knew we were on our way. But he didn't do anything, even against his will, he let us bring the human.
- Fortunately. It's not in my plans to get into a direct confrontation with him.
- Don't you think you won't win?
- It's not that. He's as strong as I am, but this girl gives him more power, so if we got into a head-to-head confrontation now, I'd be at a disadvantage... I need more time.
- As you wish.
- Take her to the salon when she arrives. I'll be there waiting for you. -he said and left the throne room.

Dark#

How did I let something like this happen?
I walked across the hall to that door. The only door in this huge palace that had never been opened. I was angry, hatred of whoever built this palace. God.
The floor trembled along with the walls more and more, as my anger grew...

She had finally arrived. Her presence was so comforting it soothed me. Strange, but now mine.
- Finally, mine.

Army#

I couldn't see anything at all. I heard something, but nothing to understand.

Something in the middle of all that darkness was calling to me. It was a very strong feeling. Explainable.

- Finally, mine. - a whisper in the air, so chilling, it danced without stopping. I looked around and nothing, but soon a light appeared in the distance, and I saw it.

I moved closer and finally saw his face.
- You?
- Me. Happy to see me?
- Where am I?
- Somewhere in Nycteus. Come with me. -He held out his hand.
- Never. - I ran in the opposite direction, but soon realized that I had never left the place.
- you're trying to run away. I won't hurt you. You know, you and I are more alike than you think.
- Don't compare me to you.
- Never. -He raised his hand and touched me. He caressed my face. His hands felt warm and something inside me vibrated.
- I'm a part of two and you're lucky you still have them. -he blurted out. - I was born from the evilness of Men...
- Don't blame them for your choices. - it was him. Lux.
- Always spoiling my good times.
- These good moments are the ruin of many...
- They deserve it and more.
- Your obsession with revenge and power...
- Envy owns them, I just do his will.
- You're pitiful. -Dark smiled.
- I spent years stuck with him, always by his side, and what do I get in return? This. He ripped my wings without hesitation...-he screamed and that place shook. - I should eliminate you all, starting with his child, Johnno.
- You can't hurt him.
- I knows. But you can't do anything to save him either.
- Neither do you, to open that door. You will live in your nightmare just like him. Forever. -he looked at me.
- You think so? Why do you think you're here in the first place? -Dark started walking towards me and I backed off.

- Don't get any closer. -I screamed and ran away but I went against that door. – Aw…
- Do you really think you're smart? Let me tell you something…
- I don't want to hear it. Just kill me if you want, but I'll never help you.
- You already did it without noticing it. -I look at the doctor and the runs started to shine, and I tried to get away from it, but as soon as it opened sometime pulled me in.
It was someone…

- You?
- Run. Don't stop running no matter what. Never stop.
- And you? I... - he was scared. Very scared.
- I... even if you don't see me, I'll always be with you.
- No... you can't...
- Go. Now.
- But...
- Go. Run and don't stop. -he yelled and I ran. I ran with all my strength, aimlessly, not knowing where I was running, but I ran.
- NOOO… -Dark yelled and the ground shook. I stopped, I looked back and saw him on his knees on the floor.

Shadows formed around me. They were here. Sentinels.
I came back to my senses and started running. Heavy chains appeared on my feet, it was hard to run and then I heard someone call me.
- Army. -and I yelled back.
- Johnno.

It was so difficult to breathe, my lungs were burning, and oxygen was barely reaching my brain... I didn't know if it was a hallucination or not, but I saw a door in front of me. The sides were locked, and I couldn't stop now.
The tears fell involuntarily, but I walked through that door and... It was weird... There were huge mirrors that formed a circle, and I was in the middle of it.

I looked one by one and there were six of them, but only in three of them did my reflection appear, the other three were out of focus, as if the reflection were undefined.
I started to hear noises, too many that were hurting my ears.

I wanted it to stop. It was so loud, so deafening...
- Run. -they shouted and I started to run once more, and I crossed one of those mirrors.

LOVELESS

(...It was so strong, my anger that, even without meaning to, everything around me was destroyed, with just a touch...)

I could feel everything shaking, as if the world were at war with itself, but then it stopped.

Wrath#

Everything was too silent, too silent that not even the sound of the bells could be heard, and it was already midnight.

I was reading my favorite book, sitting on my throne when I heard it play. I got up and went down to him. I opened the big dungeon gates and ran to it, but it no longer rang.

I looked to the side and saw her standing and looking at me as she held the phone. I knew that face. Impossible to forget the one who had challenged me on Lust's birthday. She stared at me blankly, saying nothing, not even moving. The swollen eyes revealed that she had cried a lot.

She put the phone to her ear and said something, never taking her eyes off me or even blinking... My world shook. I felt it tremble.

I put it down immediately and walked away from it, her, and that huge glass that separated us. I turned to leave, but there was no door left. I was stuck... With her...

- Open the doors to your prince – I shouted and nothing.

I looked around and there was only one door, but it was held by the glass. I went over and touched it, but I didn't hear a crack. Not even my touch could break it.

The chains on my feet and hands that now showed me that this prison had been made for me was just waiting for her. The fact that she too was in chains was a mere detail.

Army#

Trapped, she was trapped. The chains were still on my feet, I no longer had the strength to fight. I wanted this all to end.

I felt that something inside me had changed. I still heard Dark's scream dance in my skull. His back. Those marks. His wings were clipped, and I knew where they were. I don't know where, but I saw them. As he had said before he ran away, we were more alike than I could have imagined. His touch... I could still feel it. So, present in my memories, yet so far from my body.

I fell to my knees, and something broke my fall. Now an old mattress made the floor softer anyway, but it didn't make any difference the handcuffs hurt, it was as if I felt his touch. The one on the other side of the glass.

Wrath, with black hair and red eyes, wore a shirt the color of his eyes with the top two buttons undone, black pants torn at the knees and boots of the same color, hair disheveled, to live up to the name. The one I'd stood up to on Lust's birthday.

He was pulling on the chains desperately, it hurt, I know because he felt that pain too, which only stopped when he stopped too. He screamed and I deafened, even covering my ears his screams were authentic and powerful.

We were the same, facing each other, kneeling on the mattress and with the same objects on each side, all the same, as if I were his reflection.

So strange, yet familiar.

(It was me and him, like there was nothing but that glass.
Everything was real and I was the reflection of his nightmares.)

Storyteller#

Wrath was increasingly desperate. Now sitting on a wooden chair, tired of trying what he couldn't do. He looked at Army who imitated him, also in the chair.

She missed something. It was so disturbing what had happened with Dark that it was difficult to even breathe or think about something.

- Why don't you play? - Wrath asked looking at the ground. – Why did you stop playing? -He yelled and it shook, but nothing happened.
- *You heard my call, but you couldn't answer.* -someone smiled. - *No.* -he replied desperately.
- *You left me there. By myself.*
- No.
- *It was your fault… Only your…*
- No. No. No. – He covered his ears as he screamed, so he couldn't hear that voice anymore, but what he didn't know was that it was all in his head and he fell… He dropped to the ground and struggled on it until it stops.

Regrettable, deplorable. It was a pity just to look at it.

Army#

What could I do? Lux was no longer here for me. He was gone. Forever. Even not listening to what he said I could calculate the number of words screamed out of his mouth.

Every time the ground shook, I felt like we were going deeper into his nightmares, so deep that my sanity was amazingly gone. So, I got up and walked to the phone but stopped halfway. I look over and he turns to me and then to the phone. He seemed to beg me to get closer to him, I wanted to go, but then I walked away.

Wrath#

- No. No. No.-she retreated more and more. How could she do something like that to me?

I needed this. Needed it more than anything. I needed her to catch it, even if only for a second. I wanted to hear it play, even if it was my illusion...

I screamed, screamed, and will scream until I reach the other side. I felt fear hovering everywhere. That feeling that came from the other side of the glass was frightening and strong enough to split for both of us.

The world around was calm... How did I know? I had lived in it all this time... It could be hectic, violent and all the names that are used to define my person, but nothing compares to this monstrosity that crushes me with every step towards my sanity.

I crawled pitifully to the glass and sat down on the floor against it.

- Come back. -I yelled and that damn phone fell on the floor. I smiled... I laughed to myself and then laughed out loud... I screamed too. So pathetic I...

- I lost... I lost myself, my sanity... Also, my light, which must now be illuminated by the night. How I wish everything was less hectic or that I could at least control all this anger, this hatred... I can't, can I? But I wish I could... - I stopped and laughed at myself. – Who do I want to kill? -I asked, smiling wryly.

Storyteller#

- All this fear I feel is mine, right? It's so stifling here on this side. -He lowered his head once more and sighed. – I can still see that smile every time I close my eyes. The last one before we go our separate ways. -he leaned his head and on the other side Army put her hand and closed her eyes. -I wish I had been fast enough for you and strong enough to have broken the damn chains, but I let that... -a tear fell from his left eye and a mark was left. A scar...

Wrath turned at once and found Army leaning against the glass as she stared at the phone on his left side.

On his knees, he rested his forehead in that kind of evil mirror that was colder than the floor his bare feet were on. He closed his eyes and smiled. What was he thinking? He touched the glass as Army had done the last time and dragged his fingers across it until they touched the floor.

- Until now I had never heard you say such a thing. I've felt it all this time, but I've never had the courage to hear those words come out of my mouth. - Wrath blurted out. - I...
- It is not necessary. I can feel it.
- I am scared. -He shut up and waited for her to say something, but nothing.

Army#

I didn't say anything because it wasn't my place to comment on his words. It was far from who he lost or even his shadow.

- They will come for us... - I let myself fall. All those shadows that surrounded me made me dizzy.
So cold... So cold... So dark...

Wrath#

A fog had crept up shortly after she fell. The floor froze, even this glass...

- In fact, they already arrived. -she said.

Something shiny appeared in the distance, along the wall. I looked back and her reflection had turned to a shadow.

- What do we do now? How are we going to save ourselves?
- We don't save or do anything. We can't, just let me take you. -she said.
- And you?
- I walked for a long time and now I'm here. I feel like it's not me anymore. I'm missing something... A lot.
- There are two of us.
- I feel heavy.
- So do I, but somehow that weight started to disappear.
- Thankfully, at least one of us is changing for the better.
- We can get out of here first and then see you later. -she was still down, and the ice was getting closer.
- I thought you were different.
- And I am.
- Doesn't it bother you the fact that I mistreated you in front of everyone that day?
- It bothers me, but I think I've mistreated you too.
- Did you also feel that I do not belong to this world?

- I felt it. I also felt that you were about to arrive even before you did and here you are.
- I'm not. It's not me you're looking for. Those words are not for me.
- Why are you saying that? I feel your presence.

- After this, everything will take a different turn. When it's finished, you'll see that it's not me. I have nothing left of this place and I still have a long way to go…
- Why are you saying that? I can see you. I know you're not an illusion. Right? -I asked.
-…-she did not answer.
- But… I lost you during our forced break… Life forced us to stop, and you weren't there at the time of departure. –he cried. They fell out of control, but the marks were visible. – I wasn't ready, I never said I was, but I've only just realized that I need you. I always needed…
- I'm not the one you're looking for, but…
- For a moment I wanted to believe you were. It's still so present in my memories. He is somehow in you. I want to get out of this… I can't anymore…

That sound again… Is it just now that he decided to play? I looked at her who was standing looking at me and then at the phone once more and without realizing I was already running towards it. I wanted it never to stop playing, but it stopped, and I already had it in my hand. She shivered as she held him.

It was such a frightening feeling, but at the same time exhilarating. How could I?

I finally took courage and brought it to my ear.

- …. -nothing. I didn't hear anything.

She continued to look at me. She was crying. I never got tired of looking at those peculiar eyes that only she had. How could that too?

- Tell me. -I begged. - I arrived... It took a while, but I finally arrived. –I said with happiness in my voice.

She backed away. She looked back with a terrified look. I did the same, but she feared what I might find behind me.

- Army. -she said, and I froze. – My name is Army.

The name fit her perfectly, as strange as anything about her.

Army#

He smiled after saying my name. I couldn't let him find out.

It was so cold on this side that it was impossible to do anything. He was the one arriving. I never stopped feeling his presence inside me for even a second. Time seemed to have stopped so I closed my eyes and waited for him to finally arrive.

It didn't take long before I felt that heavy hand land on my shoulder.

- Finally, mine. I couldn't not come after you called me so desperately. I thought I'd never see you again after you ran away from me like that...
- I'm ready but let him go.
- Why would you do something like that?
- Because it's me you want, not him.
- You're right, but still.
- I am here. I'll go with you. Let him go. -I said and he was silent for a while.
- Let's go? - finally answered. He held out his hand and I without hesitation took it. We walked, but soon I stopped. I looked back and he was still holding the phone.

Wrath was so beautiful, even though he carried all that sin he never stopped being handsome and tempting.

- Follow the light of your soul and you will find who you are looking for. –I smiled.
- What did you do? -he hit the glass and I backed away.
- The time has come. –the ground and the whole place started to shake.

Everything was falling apart. There was nothing more that could be done. That light that was on the other side was him. I smiled with happiness. Glad he was fine.

Wrath#

What did she do? Everything was falling apart and there was nothing I could do.

- Save yourself. Just one touch from you and everything will be destroyed. Take it with you and it will be the only thing that will never be destroyed by your strength. -she said, and I saw something grow in my hands.

A beautiful red flower. It was the form of my new soul, the one she had given up so that a new one could be reborn for me.

A light hit me, and I couldn't see it.
I knew it was forever, I was saying goodbye to my regret, but I also knew I would see her again, so I didn't say anything.

"Army" -I thought to myself as I smiled.

I didn't know what was coming next, but I soon heard beautiful melodies. The bells rang loudly, and a path had appeared behind me.

- Go. Run to the end and soon you'll see the great gates of wisdom and cross them before the last toll sounds.

So, I did. I was ready to go. My steps were light, but my hope heavier than ever. Now I could walk through those great gates that opened to me…
I was in Timeless.

- *My brother.* - he said, and I saw his figure come to life and take on color. Was it him? It didn't look like… But then who was it???

OTHER

(...Even though we were distancing ourselves from each other I continued to run and now we live inside the same space but chained to each corner of that huge room. The transparent glass that separated us was like a steel shroud that separated one only single world in two. I ran to answer your call, but the glass was unbreakable and the chains that sealed that cabin with seven master keys now clung to my feet.)

 # Wrath

(...I was desperate to get out of that life. The nightmares that only you could make them insignificant now took over my nights. My sanity is on this side, when before they were side by side. The wind hitting me in the face doesn't feel the same anymore. I was ripped from you, as they ripped me from my wings and now nightmares roam this side of the glass like screaming thoughts.)

#Envy

Chapter 6

HOMELESS

(I stopped being it. I stopped being happy, naïve, sad, sensitive... I had left so many things behind right after you left, without even saying goodbye. Above all, I stopped being yours. I ran, I looked for a logical reason, but I just found the other side of the mirror. I found the one that defines me now. I walked, following the path opposite yours and found the gates to Endless.)

Avarice#

I owned all of this, I was now sitting in My Throne, in My garden of My palace. Everything here was Mine by right. Including people.

It was almost noon; the Moon and the Sun were side by side ready to switch positions.

- Sir, it's almost time for your activity.
- Who said you could call me "Sir"? -I asked without getting up

- It was you my Lord.
- New orders, now they will call me Your Highness, I am a prince.
- As you wish, Your Highness... -he said.

- No... Your Majesty because I am king. I wear a crown, so yes.... No, very old. I'm young.
- So how should we treat you?
- Sir. I am the Lord of it all. Of the lands, of the waters, of the winds, I am your Lord... - I got up after hearing a noise. There was something in the bushes, I still didn't know what it was, but I intended to find out.

I reached out and they gave me my hunting gear. Whichever creature would be mine once I caught it. I positioned my bow and arrow and waited for it to reveal itself.

It came out of its hiding place. So fast... So wild... I couldn't lose it at all, so I went into the forest and ran after it, never letting go of my hunting gear.

The forest was coming to an end and the city was almost in sight. Fireworks bursting in the air made me shiver with emotion. It was party times and all in my honor.

There were allot of people, the children ran from one side to the other, the smell of good food danced in the air and the stalls of all kinds of novelties for sale attracted those from outside and the various entertainments occupied a good part of the square.

I looked all over the place and nothing. A few people stopped to admire me, others bowed and then dispersed. Among the melodies that played, you could hear screams. People also commented on suspicious events along with the amusements.

I didn't hesitate and ran there, but I wasn't the only one running. They ran. The children played with each other from one side to the other and it disturbed me. I repositioned my bow and arrow and waited for full visibility to catch that creature... But... As soon as that place was almost empty, I saw it. It wasn't from here; I had never seen anything like it before. That look so weird. That wild appearance, but at the same time scared, caused me several types of nostalgia and at the same time shivers.

I was face to face with her, in front of the carousels. So strange... This song... I had dreamed something like this once, and every night after that it insisted on showing up.

- Sir? -Someone called me, and I looked to see who it was and when I turned around, nothing in front of me was visible.

A cloud of soap bubbles danced in the air and especially the younger ones ran after them and cheered.

I searched and continued to search with my gaze... Like my dream in an advanced state... As I chased something... something, or someone, I could not see clearly, but the feeling was the same. It was heavy. My insides had now become slightly heavy. So uncomfortable that that environment caused me chills and nostalgia at an advanced level... I ran away from that feeling... That fear... That bad dream...

Army#

I had been through so many and was heavier than lead itself. I walked around, aimless without any definite direction.
He... Those glowing green eyes... How could something like that be considered reality?
I ran even without strength; I ran even without feeling my own weight, so I let myself fall. So soft, so fragrant the floor.

(That scent had come from my best dream, waking me up, but it was the thorny arms of the nightmare that woke me up.)

I opened my eyes with difficulty and saw a sky full of angels, felt an unpleasant cold and felt death. It was so hard, it felt like it had been run over, so heavy, so destroyed inside... I let a cold tear fall.

- Awake? - someone asked. Startled, I looked to my right side and saw him.

This same person had appeared in my mind. Maybe it was just a mirage, but they were identical. Dark hair, bright green eyes. Sophisticated clothing. Black dress pants, a white shirt buttoned to the last button, a black blazer with gold daggers with a strange symbol. So beautiful, so perfect. If they tell me I'm dead, I'll believe it.

- Where am I? -I asked.
- In my palace. Where else? Can't you see such beauty?
- Why
- I saw…
- Me too.
- What is your name? I know you're not from here.
- Can you tell? I'm not the only one. -I said softly.
- Did I say something?
- No. Nothing. Got to go.
- Where you go?
- Somewhere.
- You won't. – He walked to the door. – Nobody leaves here without my order and I say no.
- Who do you think you are? - I got up and walked to him… At least I tried, but I fell halfway. These people love big rooms.
- Me? -He smiled. – I am your Lord, your Prince, your King. Avarice and you now belong to me.
- I don't think so. – You are unwilling. – I'm nobody's property, least of all yours.
- Don't call me the second person. We are not intimate. -He looked at me from below, with an air of superiority. As if it were an animal. -Don't let her out, for nothing in this world! – he said, already out of the room. Soon after, the door was closed and the noise of the key turning in the lock revived memories.

- Open the door! -I yelled and crawled over to her. - Open the door! -I yelled as I banged on it with the last of my remaining strength.

Nothing I did could change what had happened since the moment I stepped into this place or what was about to happen.

The longer I remained in this place, the more merged in it I felt.

I let myself be on the floor, lying down. I curled up into a shell and let myself be until at least a milligram of that pain passed. I closed my eyes and tried to imagine a healthier place for my sanity, but nothing but his image. How can he even imagine that I belong to him? Never.

Avarice#

Even though I was away from that room I could still hear her screams. How can a simple creature cause me so much discomfort?

I walked alone to my room and stopped right in front of the door. I lifted my right hand and led it to the doorknob, but fear ran through every nerve in my body. I was shaking… My hand was shaking as if the cold was going to give it away, but it wasn't him but the one who never left me since the beginning of my walk. Himself… Fear.

Finally, I got up my courage and opened the door. I walked in confident of myself. Full chest, head up, and sure, but soon after the door closed behind me, everything collapsed. An avalanche of mixed feelings washed over me, and I went with it.

I dropped onto the soft tiger-skin rug I'd hunted down and stayed there until my eyes closed completely and I was no longer feeling my own weight.

(… you stopped being my support from the moment I learned to walk alone.)

So much irony that it even makes me want to laugh at myself. So regrettable this situation of mine…

I opened my eyes and found myself in a place completely different from my room. It looked like a setup, maybe it was a back room. Where the only light was the one that came through the hole in the glass at the very top of the wall, in one of the corners of this place.

I walked through that space looking for a way out, but I just found a huge emptiness, like the one I felt inside of me. A pleasant, familiar scent invaded my nostrils. It came from somewhere, but where?

- Happy birthday to you... - That voice... That song... The smell... It was happening again, but it never got past this part of the dream. As if it were a repetition, as if there was nothing else but my hope of finding a way out.

I turned back and a tiny light stood out in the shadows. The music still echoed inside my ears. Soon a figure had appeared from the shadows and was illuminated by the spotlight.

She looked at me with that smile, so warm... So smoky... How? I smiled involuntarily, even without realizing it, I was already euphoric, excited to know what would come next...

That song still played, still haunted my memories. Again and again I went back to that place and wait to hear your voice, but nothing... It didn't matter anymore I could never see your reflection, your real face I don't know what it would be like, I couldn't imagine.

(The eyes cannot see something inexistent, as much as a clouded glass never reflects clearly...)

My forces were like a hot air balloon, heavy but floating. I was crawling along the ground to get to a certain destination or maybe to get away from it... that was right.
Laughter... Footsteps... Melodies.... That small storage room was now completely decorated. The entertainment was on, the smell of sweets danced in the air and voices were heard, but not a single person could see. Shadow after shadow walked back and forth.

I got up and walked around.
A force was pulling me somewhere. I didn't want to know where, but I went anyway.

Soap bubbles flew in front of me from the sky. It was like the sky was blowing them at me. So bright, so reflected from light.

- Avarice. -I heard. The same sound echoed repeatedly.

A soap bubble was coming towards me, it was bigger than the others. I reached out and it touched my finger.

It broke… Was it a breath… no, a touch of the wind… or was it a release…? I wasn't sure. Only a light appeared in front of me… no, an angel. So bright, so full of life overflowing everywhere, that I envied that strength, that feeling. I wanted it to be mine in some way or if I could at least have some of it.

- Envy does not belong to you, and it will not do you any good if you take it as yours. – someone said, and I saw that light take colors and form.
- I don't envy you. I don't want you either.
- You want something you've never lost. This strength is not mine; you are letting it go.
- Who are you?
- I'm asking, who are you? This place is mine now, it no longer belongs to you.
- I am Avarice, owner of this world
- That's not the name they gave you.
- What do you know about me? Avarice was the name the world gave me, for not knowing how to deal with my greatness. They adore me more than the one who claims to be superior to everyone. The One who is said to be greater than the universe itself. He who claims to be creator of the seven races, the seven kingdoms, the seven worlds.
- I'm referring to the name that the one Dark separated from you, gave you. The name that defines everything you once were.
- I don't know who you mean… - Even before I could blink, she was already face to face with me
- Have you met me?
- You! -was her. The creature I tried to hunt.

- Army was the name they gave me. The name that will never be forgotten, even if memory leaves me. -she smiled. She smiled at me before touching my hand and lifting it high.

I broke over and over. And right after that, they took shape, color, and life. The laughs, the steps and the voices had their owners now.

Each soap bubble was a person, it was a life... I felt strange, but light...
A bubble fell onto my palm. It was tiny. So innocent... and there it remained. With her hand she closed mine and placed her left one over them.

- You can open it. -I opened it slowly, afraid but also with some enthusiasm.
- What is it? -it was a shiny, shapeless thing, but green in color. So beautiful.
- You can't wish for something that never stopped being yours. -it was at that moment that I saw all my past. Everything I lost and now regained thanks to her

Chimes sounded and I looked at her.

- Army?
- You can go. Do not be afraid. They are there. -she smiled again.

She was so strange. I smiled and took a deep breath. I was more ready than ever. Now I knew it wasn't a dream and her reflection was already vivid in my mind.

(I didn't know you left me your soul before I opened my little hands and saw the star leap that guided my every step after your departure.)

Chapter 7

FACELESS

(...the ground shook as if the world were collapsing and my reflection had disappeared into the water.)

Army#

I was choking. I opened my eyes and found myself in the water. So far from the surface that I felt like I was about to hit the bottom and that's when I saw the light at the top, maybe it was just my illusion, but I believed it wasn't and I wanted to reach it. I swam and continued to swim, even though the top seemed unreachable.
I saw it... It was the real light. The sun, the air. It was all real.
I took a deep breath and then exhaled, the air was pure, so pure it was almost unbreathable.
I swam to shore. It was me. I saw myself reflected in those strange eyes. I didn't know how, but it was like I was facing a mirror. How can this be real?
Not to mention the strange feeling of knowing him forever, even though it was the first time we were meeting, but after everything I've seen so far, I would believe anything, even if it was a lie.

Superb#

But what creature was this from the waters, as strangely beautiful as a divinity, but with distant and peculiar scents?
She don't belong here. The dress was indeed out of the ordinary.

(I was once... maybe I was happy, where the sky was bright blue. The blue that lit up my days, but that has long since ceased to exist.
Everything I had said, someone had listened to it for you,
someone had given it more importance and held it fondly...
I suppose so, or it would be what I wanted to happen?
Perhaps yes. Perhaps among all this, you were the only color
I had seen in this black and white world of mine.
I wish I could say you were mine, but I knew right away it
was a lie as soon as I saw myself reflected in your eyes.)

Inside my thoughts I hadn't even noticed that she was already out of the water.
I walked through my garden as if it were something out of the ordinary. For me it wasn't. It was the most beautiful garden that could exist in all eight realms. It was Mine and she had her feet in it, but she walked carefully, thinking perhaps even of the fragility of the grass.

I followed her with my gaze and watched her walk towards my refuge, so without waiting a single second, I tried to stop her.
- Don't you dare invade my space.
- I want to see what you have...
- Don't make me repeat it a second time.
- Don't treat me for yourself. If I'm not mistaken, we are practically the same age.
- I know you. I don't remember ever seeing you. Now I must go. -I heard the chimes and knew that the night would soon appear. I took the forest path and walked to my palace.

Army#

He started walking into the forest and I followed him. I didn't want to be alone.
- And you never saw me, this is the first...
- I'm not interested. If you don't mind, I ask you to leave. Do not follow me.
- I don't know where I am, or where to go. I have no place to go.
- Go back the same way you came. You didn't come here from the waters? So go back through them.
- I came, but I don't even know how I got there. I can go with you...-he stopped and looked back.
- Do not look at me directly, I did not give you permission for such an act.
- I apologize. -arrogant.
- Do not follow me or I will send her to Oblivion. I won't repeat myself again. -he turned and went on his way.

I was left behind. He left me alone in the middle of the forest.
I didn't know where to go so I walked around. I walked and continued walking until I found a small reach, stopped to rest, and took the opportunity to drink water.

After some time, I went back to walking and hunger was already approaching me.
Gluttony. I smiled to think that at this hour I would be eating. How I miss him... A smell of food invaded my nostrils and I followed in its wake.
The chimes were ringing at the top and the sun was already face to face with the moon and it wasn't long before it got dark.
Midnight. The moon shone overhead, and the sky was clear. I could see the galaxy lurking.

I walked for some time, I didn't know how much, but it was some and my strength was now a metaphor. I could barely stand upright, so I dropped after a few steps and the darkness washed over me.

superb#

No matter how much I looked in the mirror I could never understand what I saw. It wasn't what I wanted it to be, it wasn't like it used to be. It was not me. There was no reflection that I could see, to remind me of my authenticity... Why?
I had forgotten what it was like after I felt the ground shake with intensity and I no longer saw myself reflected in my waters or any mirror in this realm, but for some reason I found myself reflected in those peculiar eyes...
I walked and continued to walk from one side to the other, trying to understand what was happening and nothing... Not a single sign.
Only her image appeared in my mind and in my mirror's reflection.
I left my room and went to my living room. I opened the big doors that led to the only place where I felt totally free.

Army#

I felt the cold water hit my face, I heard its drops lightly hit the ground, I heard a beautiful melody, equally beautiful, like the one Sloth used to play, but this one contained something more than just musical notes. It contained magic, something that made my heart ache just hearing the first note.
I opened my eyes and could see the angels in heaven. A heavenly image gave me the illusion of being in heaven, but it wasn't. I heard something else... A heavy, panting breath and an already familiar smell invaded my nostrils once more. It was soft and alluring, mesmerizing...
A circular room where the walls were a huge glass that covered them. The floor like mirrors of crystal-clear water.
Superb wore a white shirt and pants of the same color and fabric, maybe it was his pajamas. A light purple robe. Blond hair and eyes a bright dark purple. Like jewelry. Rings on all ten fingers and bare feet.
His hair flew as he moved to the tune. Elegant steps, full of feelings and stories. As beautiful as a fallen angel.
I couldn't stop looking, as much as I wanted to know what I was doing in that place.

The lights that formed as he danced were like stars or seemed to dangle with the universe itself. So majestic.

I got up and stayed in the same place so I wouldn't be seen, but it didn't do much good. All that magic was gone, and he stopped dancing before looking at me.
- Where did you go? -He approached more and passed right by my side. Didn't he saw me? - Why did you leave me? -He yelled and I got scared. Couldn't he see me? He was staring into the mirror, but he seemed to be looking at nothing.

How devastating it was to see him like this. I walked over to him and touched his shoulder.
- Can you see me? - I asked and he looked at me.
- What are you doing here? -he shouted again and walked away quickly, turned his back, and walked to the exit.
- Wait.
- Do not follow me? - I ran, but halfway there I fell.
- There. -he stopped. The music was still playing, and the strings were still there, but all those feelings weren't.
- Why do you insist on following me? Why can't you stay away? Follow my orders or just disappear...
- Why? Why are you so upset about my arrival, what affects you so much? The fact that I'm a stranger and no, because I don't obey you or because I somehow make you feel strange? Because if so, we are two. I don't know why but here I am.
- Didn't you want to go back?
- Yes, I wanted...
- Then go back and bring back everything you took.
- What did I take? I don't have anything that is yours...
- You took what I loved most, and you came in its place. I knew that something bad was about to come after that tremor and then you appeared, and nothing is as it used to be. Nothing that can come back until you leave.
- I already said I can't and I don't know what you've talking about. What did I steal from you that you loved so much?

- It doesn't matter anymore; I won't have it back...-he looked at the mirror and then at the floor. What did I steal from you...?
- What?
- Return.
- I can't.
- If you don't go, I'll never have it back. - he said looking all over the place. What were you looking for? I got up and walked over to him... I tried...
- Stop. Stay away.
- I can help. That's why I'm here for you...
- I don't need your help, I want you to go away. Disappear from my life, from my mind, I need you to go away. Bring him back...-he started screaming incessantly and covered his ears.
- Who?
- My reflection. All I see is complete emptiness, I see nothing beyond that, nothing, and every time I try to remember what I was like before, your image pops into my mind - he screamed and the ground shook. Everything disappeared. A shower of feathers fell on us, and the mirrors began to crack.
- Don't ever come back. -those words danced in the air and a loud noise came to further ruin the environment as soon as he closed the door and disappeared.
He was gone and had just given up any salvation I could give him.

Everything I had done so far had disappeared in a flash, with a snap of fingers. The mirrors snapped as if Wrath had touched them, the lights, the water rushed up the house at a thunderous speed, and all the light had been blown out.
I asked myself what would come next. Would I go home? And Superb? Only him was missing, but he didn't want me in his life.
How could I be the reason his reflection disappeared? Why do I have to go through this?
Something was different, he wasn't the only one to lose something I had lost it too and it wasn't something small, I just didn't know what it was yet.

(You left like you didn't want to be seen and you came back like you didn't want to be felt.)

Army#

I saw the light through my closed eyes and opened them with difficulty. The singing of birds, the sound of water hitting the rocks were some of the many sounds I could hear in the middle of that place.
It was the vision of paradise. Several trees together suggested that I was now in heaven. This was paradise for sure.
So beautiful, all those smells together, those colors. It was Haden's garden. A huge variety of fruits only reminded me of how hungry I was, so I chose the first one that was closest and ate it.

- What do you think you are doing inside my cougar, eating the fruits of my trees? -Forget it, leave heaven I'm in hell. It was him. That voice was impossible not to recognize.
- I'm eating. As far as I know, I don't see anything indicating *"private property"*.
- I thought I was clear about not wanting you around.
- I think I do not understand.
- Take her.
- Where?
- To Oblivion, as I said. -he mustn't be right in the head.
- In addition to having lost his reflection, he must have also lost his senses. -if he know what that means. I do not think so.

Some guards grabbed me by the arms and dragged me to a... cart? Was... They threw me like an animal and closed the door. I felt moved and knew he was serious.

It took us some time to get there, we had to stop at least three times, but I was always inside that damn mini prison and then we finally stopped.

The door opened and I felt, however small it was, a glimmer of hope, but that was soon enough when I came across that scene.
The air was heavy, I was barely breathing, and it was impossible to keep me sane.

Before going down I was chained like a prisoner. It was a long way there. I felt like a convict on death row.
- You can walk. -he said and I was forced to do it.

He was inside his carriage as I walked through that crowd. Two lines on the side and a space left for me to pass in the middle. It was humiliating and all for accepting to carry a weight that wasn't mine.
- I understand how you feel. I felt the same... I still feel it, whenever I close my eyes and try to think that everything is the same as before.
- I didn't say you could talk.
-I know, but every convict has last words to say.
- I don't want to hear them.
- You can listen without listening. You can ignore them, even if you don't hear them, the wind will take them to a faraway place, and you'll never remember them. -I didn't say anything so I assumed it was a *"do as you understand"*. - I thought I could carry this weight, but I was wrong. Until now I didn't know what I was missing, but now I know what I lost. I lost not only the direction I was taking, but myself as well. I looked at myself in the mirror and saw my own reflection through my eyes, but with each passing day I could no longer see it until it rose to the surface. Even though I'm not in the water, I feel like I'm sinking. Not because of their weight, but because I was careless and forgot to support my own weight as well. I met souls like yours. I met Lust, Sloth, Wrath, Johnno, Avarice, Lux and the first of you all. I took them back to the one who one day let you go and here I am, lost and not knowing what to do... -The ground shook and I stopped walking. I looked up and the sky seemed to be opening.
It would be about to touch midnight and the moon was still side by side with the sun.
- I thought I saw the world go around a thousand circles and time receded. I came from another world just to take you back and here I am...
- Enough! You can stop.
- I never had anything until I found the beginning of the road that brought me to you. I don't care if I'm going to be forgotten or if I'm stuck in Oblivion...
- I said enough! – he shouted.

- Even if your eyes have lost sight of you, your heart won't. We will always know who you really are...
- I see you don't like to hear what I say. -the carriage stopped, and the door opened.
He got out and stood in front of me, but not facing me. - I said enough!
- Why is it tormenting you so much to hear me speak? -I asked. I had nothing left to lose. It was going to be forgotten forever.
- Because listening to you is like remembering my worst nightmare.
- Do you fear the past, the present and what is yet to come?
- Don't talk about what you don't know.
- What don't I know? I know who you are, what you were, who you will be... I know what you lost and how to bring it back.
- Then tell me.
- No…-I raised my hands and asked him to take those chains off me.
- You can talk now. -finally free.
- I do not know. I just know that no matter how much you look for what you missed seeing, you'll never find it and even if it comes back, it won't be like before. What you saw through me was your reality, you saw your Self. Who you really were? What they stole from you was not your heart, but your vision. You stopped seeing you to see what they wanted you to be. A simple illusion.
- I was always like this, I have nothing to change. I'm Superb, I'm above any of you and there's no one to compare to me. I am the most beautiful, the most...
- Perfect? Was that what you were going to say? Do you feel perfect? Did you ever feel that you were?
- Now. I feel that I am all of this. It's the first time that… Everything disappeared after you appeared from the waters.
- For me you are how I see you now, how I saw you inside that place. The way you danced, was you, it couldn't be something made, created, it was genuine, it was part of you. I saw the universe dance with you, and everything was filled with magic. I saw your true Self.
- Why only you see what you say I am? Why can I only see you?
- I don't know, maybe because the eyes are the mirror of the soul? Because when you saw yourself reflected in my eyes, you saw who you really were. I can't put someone else in your place and tell you it's you. Can I?

- I stopped believing in you, from the moment I saw myself reflected in your eyes. You're not mine, you don't belong to me... As much as I want you, you won't be.
- I have no owner. I'm nobody's, but I can be your light. Your mirror. The one that will guide your steps. If I were the one from before than maybe yes, but now I can't do anything.

For the first time he looked at me and I at him, but then he backed away.

- I know you do. Either way I'm already lost. -we walked to the precipice, and he stayed farther back.
- You're having a party and you haven't even invited me? -that voice. I knew he had felt something.
- Dark.
- Lady Army.
- What are you doing here?
- I came to visit you. I haven't heard from you for a long time, and I've heard rumors that you've received visitors from outside. I wanted to know who they were.
- You are not welcome in my kingdom.
- Do not be rude. Don't forget who brought you...
- I never asked you for anything.
- I know, but I just wanted to give you a present. You're like a son to me.
- You act like a curse. You were the one who brought him into this life. He was just a child.
- I saved him before the world destroyed him… I gave you power. I gave you what you would never have if you lived the life God would give you. They all. I saved them, all seven.
- It wasn't salvation. It was a curse. They had a life before this that you say is the best there was. You painted his portrait in your image and now he lives inside an illusion. You are nothing but a shadow that will never find its light.
- I already found it and I need to erase it to be able to live.
- You won't make it.
- They are stronger now.
- I have Superb.

- I'm not yours. I have no owners. I'm the one who decides what I'm going to do.
- Sure? Will you really do what you want? What about Johnno? -What about him?
- You can't do anything to him anymore. Lux won't let you.
- Sure?
- You know me better than that. Have you forgotten? I asked and he didn't say anything.
Again, the ground shook and the sound of the gates opening was heard everywhere.
I closed my eyes and sang the melody I had heard as Superba danced. I felt something magical inside me and walked over to him.
- What are you doing? -he asked, and I opened my eyes. I could see sparkles like a purple diamond. I smiled and took his hands.
I looked at the sky and let a tear fall... Maybe the last one I had left, and all my purity had gone with it, but before falling, Superba had taken it as his and it shone brightly between his hands and the soul had blossomed.
A light had appeared in the background, and I had taken Superb's hand before I started running. We had to go through those gates, at least he had to.
We were closer and I could hear his voice calling out to us, but there was something that still weighed heavily inside me.
It was the end.
I could feel Dark right behind us, and the passage was inches away.
I stopped. Something wouldn't let me go on, my body wouldn't allow me to move one more millimeter.
- What's it?
- I can't continue.
- We're almost there. We must go now...
- You must go. I can't.
- Why? Dark is about to catch up with us.
- I know.
- So, let's go...
- I can't move. I feel heavy. I'm stuck in this place.
- You said it was the last one.

- I thought so, but someone didn't pass, there's still something missing. I can't go if you're not all together.
- I'll stay with you.
- You can't. If you stay you will be lost forever.
- So will you too. -the gates were already closing.

superb#

I still didn't understand what was happening, but I knew that nothing I said would change her mind. Not to mention that no matter what I said, she wouldn't listen to me.

- What am I going to do on the other side? How will I know if it's still me or not. How will I...
- I'll be your mirror and even if you can't see me, I'll know who you really are and whenever you see me reflected in it, you'll also know.
- I don't know where to go or what to do...
- You don't need to do anything. Just go without fear or insecurity. Don't let it stop you from doing what you feel is right. Fight as if perfection is calling you and make each battle bring you closer to it, and when you finally feel free falling, I will make you fly like a feather.
- And you?
- I'll come later, with whoever stayed behind.
- I don't want to be alone again.
- You won't be brother I'm here. You can come - I heard. I looked at the other side and a figure had appeared in the middle of the light.

I turned to her and smiled. She had done so much for me, and I didn't even know her name.
- I don't know your name.
- The Universe named… No you all did named me as Army.
- Army. Will you be all right?
- You won't even miss me.

Army#

It was about to closing and he wouldn't make it in time, even if he ran with all his strength. So, I had no choice.
Dark was close and I needed to save Superb.

"I didn't believe my eyes either until I saw me through you."

Storyteller#

(Army had felt Dark beside her and seen the last of them lose his salvation, she knew that no matter what she did, He would always be one step ahead of her. It would be her shadow.
Then Army had one last look at the sky and with what strength she had left, she screamed, and the Gates of Wisdom opened up even more, to Superb.)

OTHER

(I've dreamed of your face so many times, but it was no longer visible after I lost sight of you, I couldn't even remember it. The fogged windows... the day had been taken by night and the waters trembled. The pillow battles we did to measure strength were a simple pretext to make sure we were still together. I could feel it too... So many times, I woke up and your bed was empty. Other times I could see you, sitting on the bed while you were holding your darling pillow, but nothing happened. It was as if you were a simple mirage, and your presence could not be felt... Maybe you don't want to be found.)

#Avarice

(I saw you. I saw you farther and farther away, but I thought you were leaving me. I always looked at you from afar, but that time I couldn't see you anymore. You were out of my reach. And I filmed all your joy so that I could also feel like this... But before we got here, I started to feel empty inside. So many times, I woke up and your bed was empty. But I could never see you, whenever I arrived it was empty, and I felt that way too. Empty... So, I stopped believing that you ever wanted me by your side.)

#Superb

The Dreamless

SYNOPSIS

(You were not lost to pay for our sins, but to find us and find yourself.)

#Wrath

Once it had been a simple legend, for many, but it has long since become the reality of others…

Where did those who believed go? Those who once abandoned their dreams and now follow a path different from ours? -they all wondered, whenever they watched the kids play without any worries. So pure, so innocent, in a cruelly indecisive world.

How could that be possible?

(Once upon a time, it is no longer outside, on a beautiful planet now called Pleyades, but for humans it's just the end of the world they call Endless.

It is in the dimension parallel to theirs. Eight kingdoms have lived in peace for millennia until now.

…but what matters now is how it all started. How did the Endless legend come true?

All legends and myths have a bit of reality behind each story.

If Gods Exist? Yes, there are and as the story that we now know about Pandora tells, Zeus gave to his eldest daughter a box as a gift that would be given to Epimetheus, brother of Prometheus who lived together with humans.

I could never imagine what would be inside that beautiful box, but Zeus did and had asked his daughter that it never be opened, with the intention of encouraging them to do so.

Epimetheus ignored his brother's warnings not to accept any gift from Zeus, but Zeus ignored him and asked Pandora to open it, thus releasing the plagues her father had begged on God's creation, to challenge Him.

With the evils all set free, the Golden Age had now ended, and God's creation had lost all its perfection, but he was not satisfied yet, something would have to be done to fill that void.

Zeus had watched humanity succumb to such a nightmare and the fact of seeing them destroy each other had given him the brilliant idea of visiting his new paradise, but something prevented him from passing.

- This world doesn't belong to you. – God had told him.
- What do you think of my present? I hope you liked it. – Don't feel so comfortable. Go back to Olympus and free my children.
- Never. From now on they will worship Me as their only God. I will no longer be inferior to you
- I always considered you as a brother, but from now on I will stop doing it.
- I've never felt such a thing. You robbed me of the possibility of being respected and I just took possession of what should be rightfully mine. -God was enraged and had eliminated any attempt by Zeus to tread the Earth.
- Even if I cannot enter in Time and time again I would go back to that place and wait to hear your voice, but nothing... my new paradise, you will never have your creation back to perfection. -he smiled and went up to Olympus.

Revolted by such an attitude Zeus continued to stalk humanity day and night and with each passing year he realized that no matter how hard he tried, his goal would never be fulfilled, so he acted.

One afternoon when the sun would unite with the moon, on the first day the year, Zeus had decided to peek one last time on Earth and not far from the garden of Haden, a beautiful woman danced to such a precious melody and under a tree in a small basket placed in the shade a small soul slept inside.

It was the child she had carried inside her... It was her child.

- Such preciousness should be destroyed. I will not allow anything to steal my greatness or be compared to me in any way. -Long before he could reach his goal, something from the shadows had appeared to him - Why erase it when you can use him as second eyes down here? God does not allow you to pass, but he is already here. Nothing better. – Persuaded the serpent, but soon it took shape and a being in black, completely covered up to the head, knelt before Zeus.

- Who are you? I've never seen you before.

- I came to help. My name is Dark. I like to be discreet, but I've seen you a lot. I see how dedicated you are to your latest creation; I also saw how challenging it was. A God with your greatness. May I help you; I know how to do it.

- Why would you do that? What do you want in return? -He asked suspiciously

- I don't want anything, just to stay with someone who values me and who shares the same ideas as I do. Only that. Once I was the one God trusted the most, but after another appeared, he discarded me as a simple seed that will never grow on any ground.

- What do you suggest?

- I saw that during all these years you still haven't reached that goal. You destroyed something that was already created, why not start from the beginning? - he pointed to that sleeping being. Fascinated with such an idea could finely start a new Era.

Not long before the change of year, Zeus had asked that strange being to bring the child to his presence and so it happened.

When the sky opened and the universe peeked out, the moon and the sun merged as one, Zeus put his hand on that little head and said:

- I Zeus, as your new God, I grant you the privilege of possessing such a gift. To you, pure child, I offer my home like yours from now on, and from this moment on nothing on Earth will be able to be compared to you, you will live like a prince… My first creation. The Universe will call you Superb, whose name will never be forgotten in any millennium. You will live forever and ever. -and so, it was.

Merope, the first kingdom had been credited,
and the first of them was born.

It was a party. For weeks, everyone on Olympus celebrated.
In the midst of so much joy and satisfaction Zeus had
forgotten that he had placed a single Virtue inside the box
and that she too would now be free in the world.

On the other hand, God had not forgotten and was preparing his attack.
– Did you call me? -I asked as soon as I arrived in his presence.
- I did.
- I see they still celebrate. What do you plan
to do about it, Father? -I asked…

Who am I?
I'm the one Dark was referring to when he
said he was replaced by someone.
My name is Lux, I came before Rafael. I also lived on Earth
for a while, but I came up soon after chaos had set in.

- Due to such ambition Zeus forgot that he had delivered the
only salvation that brought my most perfect creation to ruin.
- What should I do?
- Seek secretly a soul to carry it.
- Don't you think it will be too heavy such a burden to carry a lifetime?
- I know, but only someone with a pure soul can
restore peace to this world, and save those who didn't
had a chance to choose their own destinies.
- I understand. -I went down and started my searches.

*(It wasn't because His upbringing was imperfect that it
brought hem to ruin, because it wasn't, but because Zeus
wanted to compare himself with the incomparable.)*

Now Superb, the child who grew up beside Pandora, but living on
Earth, was grown up and as a gift for his upcoming birthday, Zeus had
asked him to choose the second child who would carry another evil.

- My most beautiful creature, I grant you the wish to choose the one who will accompany you for eternity. -he said and the child smiled.

He had left the gardens and run in search of a companion. That's when he heard beautiful and nice songs and smells, not far away. A little scared but with joy that he would have some company. So, he went.

He lurked beside an amusement and had seen such a light and joy-filled one. A child not much older than him, he was playing hide and seek with someone and was instantly enchanted by him. He was dazzled that he hadn't even noticed he was looking at him.

- Do you want to play? Let's play. -he smiled at him and Superb pulled his hand away.

Pandora looked at them and watched them, she already felt him as hers.

- Why do you walk away? -the boy asked Superba after he had let go.
- I need to go.
- Why don't you stay a little longer? That way we can play without stopping.
- I must go back. You also need to go back.
- I have no place to go back, I have nowhere to go.
- Come with me and you won't feel alone. -Superb had extended his hand and he held it tightly. He had looked up and begged him to be his mate.
- Father, let this be my second child. – Pandora asked him.
- To you, whose nothing you have, I will give you everything you desire and from now on you will be called Avarice. The world will be yours and no one else. You will buy and fill yourself with endless riches. Nothing will compare to you. -that was how the second prince and the second kingdom, Alcyone, were created.

It wouldn't take long for the seven to be incarnated and I was still looking for Hope.

I walked for days and saw places that didn't exist before, I also
met people who evil had never possessed. Among them a survivor
and discovered that within a few moons she would give birth.

- Lord, voice that you are full of light, help me and protect
those who are about to come into the world. – I begged
while she held my arm with all her strength.
- Do not fear. Nothing will happen. God is with us.
- Not with me. Not anymore. I let myself be carried away by desires and
became a sinner. I'm impure, I don't want this child to pay for my sins.
- God will be with her. -I knew she would be the one
to carry that fate, but i couldn't say anything.

Meanwhile one more child would be converted.

Victim of cruel fate, she had been separated from his youngest
and was desperate to find him again. With the heart in her hands,
Pandora had taken him into her arms and taken him to her father.

- My father, to you I present this poor child, whose life was
unfair and had taken from him the one he loved most.
- What do you want? -she asked the boy and he in tears said:
- Nothing more than the one that was taken
away from me. I want him back.
- Then to you, I will give you all the strength that holds
within you. From now on you will be called Wrath and the
world will fear your strength. You will destroy everything
wherever you go and whoever destroyed you one day. It
was the third prince and the third kingdom, Maia.

Several moons passed and the world fell further into disgrace.

The festivities on Olympus would be far from over. The
year was about to end, and time was getting shorter.

One more had been chosen.

A slave to life, he had had to know hard work from an
early age to be able to feed his younger brother.

Dark had taken him to Zeus's presence and told his story,
as a birthday present, he had called his daughter.

- My dearest, to you, I give you the fourth child
so that you can take care of him.
- I can't accept it, I must go back, my brother is waiting
for me, I don't have anything to feed him.
- Then bring him to me and feed him. -and so, it was. –
What do you want in exchange for such a kind offer?
- I do not want anything. I will only give you a new home, here you
will not lack for anything. To you I will give eternal rest, you will
never have to remember the meaning of the word work. You'll have
someone to do it for you and your youngest, I'll give you all the
wishes that life can offer you. You will live on pleasures and only for
them. Two more kingdoms were created, Taygete and Sterope...

There were only two left and Dark always back and forth.

From a distance I saw each of them ascending, but I could
do nothing. She would be born within a few moons,
not many, and her existence was still a secret.

It was night and the stars were shining brightly above our heads.

Everyone was asleep and I was beside her, a force was dragging
me into a deep sleep, and I had closed my eyes involuntarily.

*("I had had a vision, the vision that we would walk together
into the sunset, and you would be our way. I had also
seen the world fall to ruin after your departure.")*

I had woken up with the rays hitting me directly
in the eyes and had lifted me up.

The dream wasn't mine; she had given me fragments of her future. Now she realized to me that it was not us who had chosen her for such a fate, but fate itself had been chosen by her. I smiled and looked up at Heaven. Father had also seen and encouraged me.

While on earth we prepared for the arrival of the savior in Olympus Superb always disappeared. Where would he be? Dark knew, as he watched him closely.

Superb stood by the garden of Haden, leaning against a tree.
– What are you doing down here? Your mother is looking for you.
– I'll be up soon. -he answered.
- Her royalty, she sent me up with Your Highness. I will not be able to come before Them without a you.
– I know how to go alone. You don't need to come.
- As you wish. -Superb went back and Dark before climbing heard something through the trees.

Walking in the shadows he had spotted a boy a little older than the princes. He ate one of the cougar apples, trying not to get caught.

- What do you do? This cougar belongs only to Superb, prince of all beauty and perfection.
- I didn't have anything to eat. I didn't want to dishonor this place with such a sin. -without saying anything Dark climbed with him and took him to the presence of his God.

-Your greatness, almighty Zeus, I bring you an intruder. He stole apples from Haden's Garden.
- What do you have to say about such an accusation?
- Nothing. I'm guilty. I was hungry because all the food I had was stolen from me by strange people and the one I had found was spoiled.
- Poor child. So thin and helpless. Father, forgive his sins and let me take care of him as mine.
- So be it my daughter. To you I give you the sixth child. You will call him Gluttony, the one whom hunger had once welcomed, but who from today will leave such a word in ignorance. He

will eat and drink what he please in this world. He will have the most powerful palate and the most delicate tastes. The sixth kingdom was born, but the name remained in oblivion.

Even though he was now Prince Gluttony, he had never completely forgotten about his former life.

The six lived on earth and created their own kingdoms, but God would not allow that to happen much longer.

Finally, that day had arrived. The day the savior would come into the world. The last day of the year had also arrived.

Zeus had discovered that God was looking for Hope and had visited him.

- Are you here to inform me that you've changed your mind?
- I will never give up my creation as you did with yours.
– What did you came here for? Is the feast on Olympus over?
- It's just getting started. I came to say that I already have six of them. I also know that you are looking for it, but I warn you that you will not find it.
- Why are you so afraid? You know very well that I will and that that day is near, closer than you can imagine.
– I won't let her live.
- Nothing will happen to that child while I exist but try and you will prove my power.

God had given up trying to convince him to take them off Earth.

- Now go down and hide in Olympus and never come back. You will not be welcome here. -and Zeus went.

Then God had closed his eyes and stretched his right hand over their heads and said:

- Here I will create Prime, for those who want to follow the path to me. -He had lowered his hand and laid it on the Earth. – Here it will be Timeless, so you can choose the path you want to follow.

At last, he had raised both hands and beneath his feet a crack had split the ground and said:

- Here will live your creation. I will call this place Endless and all those who follow Sin will live and will never know what is good and will look to the light, standing by their side. From now on, at every stroke of midnight, from the last day of the year, until the rest of its existence, your creation will sink deeper and deeper into itself and will never find its way back. They will live in their deepest regrets until the light rescues their souls and brings them back to me.

After Zeus left, I appeared with two little souls in my arms. – Here they are.

He had turned to me and placed his right hand on their little heads and blessed them.

- To you, Hope, I will deposit all the willpower that may exist in the seven corners of the universe, there will be no harm that can consume you, nor any force more powerful than that which you carry, and you, now her eldest, will have forever what so much you have protected until now, there will be no goodness like yours, even if evil merges with you, you will cease to be who you are.
- Father? -I wanted to ask something, but I don't have the courage to ask.
- Lux.
- My father? Thank you for everything you've done for my kids. They are my brothers, and it is also my home.
- Now you can go down and take care of them like your firstborns. Go baptizes them. Gives them a name and watch them grow. Whenever you want to return, the doors will always be open. -here was the answer to my question.
- What about Dark? Even knowing that Zeus cannot leave Olympus he will be his eyes. However, one of them is still missing.

- I know. As for the last one, there is nothing we can do. Protect them for now. Give them life. A story. A reason to continue even if it's without you.
- So, I will.
- Lux?
- Yes?
- Don't let her remember or let him forget her, don't let her grow up with him or remember his existence until their next meeting. Take her away, but only he can get through. When the time comes, you will come back to me and leave them behind.
- As you say, my father.

After that I went down and hided with my newest kids. Time passed and even living a turbulent era they grew healthy and far from temptation.

On the other hand, while everyone played away from the gardens of Superb, the youngest of them, Lust hid from the others and was the only one who had not yet been found.

- Lust? - Shouted one of them, but the youngest didn't answer. It had been some time since the game had started and he should have appeared by now.
- Lust? - they continued to call him and nothing. He was beyond their reach, almost near a beautiful place where everything was too perfect to be real, a great place for Superb.

He walked for some time and saw wonders he could only find on Olympus.

- What are you doing around these parts? -A slightly husky voice woke him from his thoughts.
- My apologies. Where is this place?
- Somewhere out there. Not many people visit this place and those who leave never come back. Are you passing through?
- Let's say yes.
- Are you looking for something specific?

- An outlet. I need to get back to my people,
they must be looking for me.
- Always follow that path and soon you will find the exit.
- Appreciate. -Lust followed that path and was more and more certain that something like this could not exist on earth, but he did not want to question his eyes and continued the path. On the other hand, his brothers had also found such an earthly paradise.
- You could live here Superb. -stated Sloth.
- I do not believe. Nothing compares to my home.
Nowhere in this world can be compared to mine.
- Then I could conquer these lands. Superb doesn't want them. I will keep them.
- Sorry, but these lands do not belong to anyone, nothing or no one can take them as theirs. -they were startled by the lady who appeared from behind.
- Do not mind. He was just kidding. -Gluttony tried to ease the tension.
- As a matter of fact, I was not, but maybe another time.
- Come on, we must find Lust and go home. -
Wrath was out of patience.
- Are you looking for a handsome young man with strange clothes like yours? -she asked, and they looked at her almost offended.
- Yes, we are, have you seen him around here? -again, Gluttony was the only one who seemed calm.
- Yes, I've seen him. It went that way. -she showed him the way and he went.
- Thanks a lot for the help.
- You're welcome.
- When I find him, I will make him regret having made me come here.
- I won't let you hurt him. You won't lay a finger on him. If you're mad at something, read your book or destroy something of yours. -Sloth stopped and faced Wrath head on.
- I knew this game was not a good idea.
- Nobody made you come or play.
- Could you stop. Our mother watches us. Let's look for Lust and then go home.

-Superb almost shouted and everyone continued their way. Up ahead, the youngest was looking intently at something.

He was standing in front of a mysterious door far from everyone, almost out of town. He didn't understand the reason, people passing by or trying not to go through those parts, he felt more like going there.

Perhaps it was because of the sensation that aroused them as they approached the forest that was a few steps away. It was like heaven, as beautiful as the gardens of Superb, but a beauty that shuddered to panic itself.

- What are you doing here? Do you know how far we had to walk just to find you?
- Wrath, stay calm. You don't need to yell at him.
- Superb?
- I won't repeat it again.
- Look. -he said and the others looked.
- What is it now?
- Notice how they get away from that door? What could be on the other side?

A black door with strange designs etched into it separated them from the unimaginable.

Gluttony felt it wouldn't be a good thing, but before he could alert them, the youngest was almost twitching face to face with it and the others followed him.

- I can feel that it is something different from what we felt before arriving here, everything else has a lighter, happier air. – he said almost fascinated by the unknown.

He reached out and touched the handle of that door and then turned it, so slowly, so carefully and its creak sounded everywhere and there were few who could hear it, but the most important...

A heavy air and everything that was opposite
to that place made them shiver.
That vision was so cruel that even without noticing
the tears fell down their heavenly faces.

How could something like this happen in such an earthly paradise like this? How could they leave something so harmless in such a situation?

Pandora saw and she even fell into despair and almost a waterfall formed in her eyes. She wanted to hold him, wanted to protect him, wanted him as her own. She wanted to give him everything he never had, everything the humans took from him and without a second thought went to Zeus.

- My father. You saw such cruelty. From an innocent soul they took everything, from him they took the perfection that is now the place they live, he was punished for the mistakes of others and locked in the darkest place of all. I want it to be mine, I want him to be my last child, I will call him Envy and from them he will take all the perfection and happiness that that place has, he will be everything he ever wanted to be, and nothing can ever satisfy such a craving. He will take everything from others, and no one will be able to blame him or even judge or take away what from now on will belong to him. -he was satisfied by such hateful words, and she saw it in his gaze. Happy and angry with humans Pandora looked at her other children and said:

- You who are now vulnerable I welcome you as my seventh and last child. From now on I will be your mother, I will protect you from all who try to do you any harm.

After that they were all together, then the youngest stretched out his hands and with a smile on his lips he told him:
- The cruel world in which you lived has ended and a new one awaits your arrival. -He smiled and held his hand firmly.

Gluttony's heart trembled, and doom was on their way.

They all went back, and Envy followed behind and the door closed. Everything else began to disappear, the colors, the perfection, the happiness, everything was now just a memory that they wanted to recover at all costs and had no choice but to succumb to the evils.

God had seen and thought a great deal after that and then told those who inhabited his children's land.

- My children. I will let you live in these lands. From them you will enjoy all its gifts. From them you will have food, water, and comfort, so it will be throughout the year. All of you will live according to your wishes, you will live as humans and at the last day of the year you will leave these lands. From them you will no longer have food, water, and comfort. -all heard these words and ignored them, because they knew that it would still be a long time before that day comes. – You will not return until the doors open again for you. You will mourn until the end of your sins and then you will come back to me, and I will open my arms and I will welcome you into them, my children. Until then I will mourn your departure.

It became night and then day came, and night came again, and it was like that for days and weeks.

Including the children of Pandora and all those who evil possessed without mercy, they would live in the lands of God. For a year they all lived as humans, they forgot they had ever known Zeus or Dark even Pandora, who had never forgotten them and who always watched over them from Olympus.

Time passed and they grew up, had a name, a home and created their own stories, all together they moved hearts, created new dreams and a future full of promises, but the oldest of them never forgot the words he heard from heaven and dreaded its coming. That's when in the blink of an eye, as if a breath had brought the future so quickly, that not even the first breath had ended.

That day had unfortunately come for all of us.

It was noon and the moon was already in sight with the sun. A white robe had fallen from the sky and then six more. It was the flood. The end of the world.

The human being had remembered the words that God had said and had fallen into despair. The ground shook and the oldest of them watched it all happen without being able to do anything. Day and night had merged, the universe had come together and embraced humanity.

Pandora in tears because was not able to take them back to Olympus, regretted their departure. They were her children. The ones she had loved so much all those years.

The oceans dried up and everything that existed on earth turned to dust. The air thinned and it became impossible to breathe. That place had become uninhabitable, only for humanity. God punished not his creation, not his children, but he drove out the unworthy, those who were succumbed and would later show the way back to those who went up to Prime.

The Gates were finally opening, and everyone could hear such a melody. Trumpets played in the skies and the beginning of the walk was announced, it was time to leave.

At the beginning of the line that was forming, Superb was the first of them, who had started the walk towards Timeless. Soon after, Avarice followed in his footsteps, Sloth let go of his youngest's hand and then followed ahead of Lust. Wrath with every step he took left its mark on the ground, Envy tried to get ahead of everyone and Gluttony still didn't have decided yet what to do.

Placed in the queue. All of humanity followed them until the last of them was about to pass and then Gluttony decided to start walking. He had run and kept running, but he knew it was too late for him to enter. The gates had already closed, both those of the overworld, Prime, and those of the underworld, Endless and he was the only one who had been lost in Timeless.)

OTHER

(It was the end. I knew it was.
I tried to go after them, but I had already lost my way since the first one had crossed through the Great Gates.
It was all done. I had already accomplished what I had come here to do, but that wasn't how I felt. Something still weighed heavily inside me. There was something that held me to that place.
My willpower was also great, and I thought I could go with them, but I had done everything to get them all through the gates, but there was someone who hadn't.
I looked to the other side and saw all the ones who would already be saved, except the first one of them all. The one who once reached out to the shadow that now keeps them company.
Maybe I was also to blame. The youngest decided to give his brother's turn, thinking he had no right to such privilege, blaming himself for everyone's misfortune, even yours.
Why did he need to stay behind if that was my mission? I was the one who should be with Him... For Him. It was my soul he wanted; it was me he wanted so much he craved. Even being here I still feel him close, it's just not visible to my eyes. I didn't know it, but now I can confirm it, we are equals. I was no longer sure who I was after I lost Lux. He did disappear because of me.

It wasn't me anymore. I had stepped into hell on my own feet. Inside, nothing was lit anymore. I tried in every way not to be succumbed to the darkness, but I don't think even I could escape it. I found myself between despair and oblivion, madness, and insanity. I saw time running right beside me and I stayed in the same place as I went crazy slowly. I also found myself between evil and cruelty... I saw, even if in an illusion, each one with their backs turned, but I saw them. It was a choice, perhaps the same one you went to subject. I had to choose between one and the other, but which one would it be? Lux? I would give anything to see him, but if I chose him, I would be leaving Dark behind and I felt that he should be my choice. I was already walking even without giving account and my choice were already made. You stayed behind because you wanted to save them, I went to Dark for the same reason. Turns into Lust the desire to want to master your own heart and to own its steps. I want to feel the reality, open my eyes again and look at all of you, as you did on the day of your departure. But this time with no regrets or any kind of hurt, just full of new hope. Who knows? I'm not saying goodbye, because we'll be meeting soon, along with Envy and Lust.

#Army

(I also felt it.
When you stepped on the other side of my mirror to an unknown place, I knew you'd already be lost, you wouldn't go back the same way if you wanted to.
It was my fault. I made you carry a weight greater than bearable, and you were crushed at the first touch, but I never imagined that the weight of my guilt was this great.
I will never blame you for your decision. Hearts weigh because we still have a soul, we still feel and somehow, he still holds your purity, brighter now as the shadow that is now beside you.
Lust lived, desired, had the best and the most pleasure, and now lives like the human he always was, before we were dragged into this disaster.
You just don't know how and what to do, so you need Him to guide you.

I know perfectly well how this feeling is, I carry it with me to this day. I'm not complete yet, I lack something. Them, the ones who are still there and more... The center of our circle is missing, the line that gives shape to the constellation dent. The star that lights our way is missing, the one that came down to light us after the moon merged with the sun.

After you left, I had this dream, I joined them. Where everything was real, it wasn't the same as before, but it was the beginning of something new, something big, and I could hear the universe scream our name so loud that the ground beneath our feet shook. We were euphoric... We were alive... We were in perfect harmony. We were one with you. Right in front of us as our shooting star, the source of our wishes. We saw Army with open arms and finally we all walked together towards a real dream.)

#Gluttony

Milton Keynes UK
Ingram Content Group UK Ltd.
UKHW010251130324
439347UK00005B/76